Vital Signs

Tessa McWatt was born in Guyana, and moved to Canada with her family when she was three. She is the author of five earlier novels; her second, *Dragons Cry*, was a finalist for the Governor General's Literary Award for Fiction and the City of Toronto Book Award. She developed and leads the MA in Writing: Imaginative Practice programme at the University of East London. She divides her time between London and Toronto.

ALSO BY TESSA McWATT

Out of My Skin

Dragons Cry

There's No Place Like ...

This Body

Step Closer

Vital Signs

TESSA McWATT

Illustrations by

ALEKSANDAR MAĆAŠEV

✳ WINDMILL BOOKS

Published by Windmill Books 2013

2 4 6 8 10 9 7 5 3 1

Copyright © Tessa McWatt 2011

Illustrations by Aleksandar Maćašev

Tessa McWatt has asserted her right under the Copyright, Designs
and Patents Act, 1988, to be identified as the author of this work.

Grateful acknowledgement is made for permission to reprint from the following:
'Four Quartets' in *The Complete Poems and Plays of T. S. Eliot*
by T. S. Eliot, Faber & Faber, 2004.
'Like a Hurricane' by Neil Young, 1975. Courtesy of Silver Fiddle Music,
Wixen Music Publishing.
'Il Mio Mondo' by Umberto Bindi, 1963. Courtesy of Anne Rachel Music Corp,
Warner/Chappell Music Inc.

First published in Canada in 2011 by Random House Canada,
a division of Random House of Canada Limited, Toronto

First published in Great Britain in 2012 by William Heinemann

Windmill Books
The Random House Group Limited
20 Vauxhall Bridge Road, London SW1V 2SA

Addresses for companies within The Random House Group Limited can be found at:
www.randomhouse.co.uk/offices.htm

The Random House Group Limited Reg. No. 954009

www.randomhouse.co.uk

A CIP catalogue record for this book is available from the British Library

ISBN 9780099538295

The Random House Group Limited supports The Forest Stewardship Council
(FSC®), the leading international forest certification organisation. Our books
carrying the FSC label are printed on FSC® certified paper. FSC is the only
forest certification scheme endorsed by the leading environmental organisations,
including Greenpeace. Our paper procurement policy can be found at:
www.randomhouse.co.uk/environment

Printed and bound by CPI Group (UK) Ltd, Croydon, CR0 4YY

For John B.

Who then devised the torment? Love.
Love is the unfamiliar Name
Behind the hands that wove
The intolerable shirt of flame
Which human power cannot remove.
  We only live, only suspire
  Consumed by either fire or fire.

"Little Gidding"
Four Quartets, T.S. Eliot

ONE

It has come to me like a dog comes to its master: tail curled between hind legs, wet muzzle nudging to be forgiven for its very existence. This thought has come: I am not worthy of her.

Anna is wearing an electrode cap. Eighteen ultrasensitive electrodes are listening to her brain, translating the signals of the synapses to numerical pulp for Dr. Mead's diagnosis. He stands before a terminal and monitors the tiny shocks of meaning. He ticks off boxes on a chart. I am slain by the look on Anna's face that says that this is how we end up, this is how the rakes of decades gather the scatterings of a single being: poorly.

"The hummingbird is nursing," Anna says, and Dr. Mead nods, taking more notes. When he asks her how many children she has, her answer is, "Thirty-four," and I try to decipher if she means three or four, perhaps counting the one that she miscarried after Fred, but I think this is reaching on my part. She has said thirty-four.

Dr. Mead makes more markings on his chart. When he finally releases Anna from the grips of the machinery, his face is sombre.

"If you see the receptionist, she'll line you up with a few appointments."

"What kind of appointments?" I ask.

"A range of different tests. I deal with the neuropsychology of these kinds of speech patterns, but . . ." He hesitates. "I'm going to refer her. We'll send you some details. If you take a seat for a moment, Theresa will come and get you."

Dr. Mead is the type of man who can smell rain approaching.

Afterwards, in a café on Bloor Street, Anna's hands tremble with a will to order, as if to hold a sentence in them and lay it out flat along a plane of reason. This is not impossible, but she doesn't know that. Instead she picks up her glass of lemonade and drinks.

"Cold eating child," she says and grimaces, knowing from the expression on my face that it didn't come out right. I nod and doodle on my napkin with the marker I use when reaching for an image, and so I draw a figure of a child on a seesaw. I know she means that the lemonade reminds her of something in her childhood, and I smile to try to reassure her that I've understood. Lemonade is her favourite refreshment, and she likes hers sweetened with the darkest of demerara sugars. I sip my beer, knowing that she won't challenge me over this early drink for fear that nonsense will spew forth from her mouth. These little advantages I now take, and my vileness bounds over fields, ears and leash flapping in spring breeze.

The drive up Highway 400 toward home is filled with a silent hum of regret, but I believe it's only mine. Anna seems calm, staring out at the sprawling commercial complexes that make all of this area between the downtown we have just left and our farmhouse an hour away seem like part of the same, flabby city that cannot seem to contain itself.

A shoulder bone. It was the empty curve that did it—her blondeness and the bones, nothing more, I swear.

"Did you call Sasha back?" I ask. Our youngest is the one who makes her laugh the most. Sasha's mere presence is like a promise that the universe has balance.

"No," she says, and shakes her head, but smiles at her daughter's name.

I wish that I had access to a sketch pad and my pen. I vow to carry them with me from here on in. There is an obvious sign for Sasha—for the poise with which she stirs the air, on stage and off. Sasha is our wind whistling in trees. I step on the accelerator, signal and pass the slow truck in front of us.

The other two are more problematic, graphically speaking. Fred, the eldest—more like my father than even his name suggests—would be something that evokes a job never quite finished or a race perpetually run. There's a glitch in his stride. Whatever it is he's running toward, his efforts seem more like duty than fulfilment. Charlotte, middle child and the most difficult, is the one I know the least but suspect I am most like. She is selfish and proud, like a statue, but she too has a contour I must work out.

I've done this secretly in my time—fangled signs for everyone I know. I wonder, if Anna loses all her linguistic abilities, whether this kind of expression might be a way forward or, rather, a way back—to small, quiet moments of clarity between us. But I would have to work faster than I ever have before.

In my years as a partner in the design firm, I had the leisure of being my own boss, and knowing that good design took time. How I enjoyed the slowness of creating shapes, even when computer programmes took over. For there is still deliberation in digital imagery. The manipulation of individual pixels is not dissimilar to the slow, exact marking of pen on paper. Eventually, though, the business ran faster than I could, and so I sold my share of the company and went freelance. Then I had to work harder to make a living, and as I worked, my family morphed into fat, vacant shadows. Lately, the work has slowed, so most of my time is now my own. In six short years I turn sixty-five (am I really only a blink away from the pasture?) and I will stop altogether. And then what?

I had envisioned us travelling. For years Anna and I denied ourselves, saved for all the eventualities that have indeed arrived, and invested everything in our children. Even so, Fred—have I unconsciously pressured him into being more successful than I was?—has a medical degree that is of little use in solving the malfunction in his mother's wiring.

"An aneurysm," Fred said, flatly, in the composed tone all doctors learn in their final years of study. "She has an aneurysm," he repeated, as though he had diagnosed her himself, ignoring the fact that Dr. Mead had already explained the condition using the same word. But then Fred is not a neurologist. I put my foot down at financing advanced degrees for any of them, so Fred is a general practitioner, and bitter, I sense, that he isn't better able to help his mother now.

Still, expert or not, Fred has reaffirmed what in all likelihood is happening to Anna: a strained and seeping aneurysm in the anterior communicating artery. It's possible that the arterial wall has always been defective, but at some moment in the last few months, blood started to drip into her frontal lobes. It's that moment I wish I could return to, to catch her, to stand stalwart against the leak—or at least to crawl inside her now and press my hands against that arterial wall to shore it up against further damage.

There, behind the office building, she whispered that I didn't need to be afraid.

"Sweet keys of sun in the dusk of the toaster," Anna said one morning at breakfast. I looked up at her, briefly, but made nothing of it, distracted as I was with the morning paper. The day continued quietly as we went about our routines, and other things she said didn't cause concern. But in the afternoon, as she came in from the garden and wiped her shoes on the mat, she said, without looking up, "Fissures on the hummingbird's feet." Although I reasoned with myself that she might be puzzling something out, I felt a quiet alarm. "Turn up the jet trails; there are steam engines and poor magpies; useless to try to do anything about them," she blurted out that evening, as she sat at the table while I took the roast chicken out of the oven. I looked up then, feeling the heat through my oven mitts. She put her hand over her mouth.

"What was that?" I asked. She shook her head and we sat down to a silent dinner. I thought she was angry with me, but when I asked her she smiled to reassure me.

Anna and I have always been comfortable with silence. The first time I acknowledged it to myself was one long afternoon, nearly thirty years ago, in my Clinton Street apartment. We had exhausted ourselves with each other, drinking one another's breath, my hands and tongue probing the curves and crevices of her olive skin, my own body a starved, chalky spade digging, digging to be nearer to her until we lay still. On rising, we spent the rest of the day contentedly washing, reading, cooking— all without speaking.

When Sasha left home two years ago, we greeted the return of our solitude and its silences with some relief. It wasn't unusual for us not to speak for long periods, and it was no different that day when Anna first uttered her involuntary riddles. She had gone to bed before me, slept soundly and risen silently to make breakfast for us both. But the dusk on the toaster, the fissures on the humming-birds, and the poor magpies could not go unexamined.

"How are you feeling today, Anna?" Dr. Mead asked her on our first visit. The same question had been asked by our family doctor a few days earlier. Upon hearing Anna's answer, he had made an emergency call to Toronto Western's neurology unit.

"I'm fine, I'm fine, the tortoises have lain and are crawling slowly and singing the song for six trees that run through the garden, and we could have dinner on the lawn, but Mike has brought the car and if the teeth are cleaned then we all . . ." she paused, looking, I believe, at the astonishment on Dr. Mead's face, and then turned towards me.

Everything went quiet. Dr. Mead reached for his ophthalmoscope; I looked into my lap, guiltily. Anna held her breath as though to cut off oxygen to the nonsense.

Or rather, I thought it was nonsense at the time. More and more every day I find myself drawn into the puzzle of her speech, determined to unravel meaning in each sentence, because now I'm sure it's there, if I only listen to her in a way I have failed to listen for thirty years.

According to Dr. Mead, what Anna has been doing, and continues to do with increasing intensity, is to compress all of her life moments into one when she speaks. Confabulation, he has told me, stems from a problem of self-definition in time. When she's with me or the children she seems less scattered about the decades, but what I hear when she's with Dr. Mead is language scrambled in a time machine. "What's your name?" Dr. Mead asked her on our first visit. "Me? I'm Anna Tractor, of course," and then she looked at me, wanting me to confirm that she hadn't ever taken my name—she was not that kind of woman—and that she was indeed Anna who went by her maiden name. But that name is not Tractor.

Anna's first name is really Aygül. Aygül—the rose of the moon, in Turkish. It became Anna somewhere along the journey as a baby from Istanbul to Toronto in the 1950s. She grew up as Anna Yilmaz in a row house in the west end of the city, near High Park, and was raised like many immigrant children to be obedient, grateful, humble. Anna told me when we first met that Yilmaz means "never give up." This moon rose is nothing if not unyielding. She is a vibrant, eccentric and intelligent woman. She has nothing in common with a tractor. Undoubtedly the light of my life, she is, of course, the curse of it as well, because there have been many days over the last three decades when I believed that without her and the drone of married life and fatherhood I might have lived something magical. I know all the clichés of my "coulda been a contender" regret, but most days I sense that she was my last brilliant choice. Since then I have made choices that have diminished who I was meant to be and what I was meant to have.

Now I must count on Dr. Mead to perform magic: mend the tear in her brain and give my wife back to me, whole, linear, complete. But he is a theory man, not a surgeon, and confabulation is a tricky foe. From a Stayner library book called *Brain Fiction*, I know that confabulators have problems with context. While they appear to have a grasp on their autobiography, it's a slippery one, like a driver's control of a car on a snowy highway. Memories drift, swerve, and can skid into a pileup.

When Charlotte was fifteen and we let her go out to a movie with that boy who had teeth too big for his lips, "No!" I said to the teeth and the boy. "Gentle," you said to the fifteen-year-old in me who had not known how to treat a girl. When she came home I hugged her, and asked if she'd enjoyed the movie. You— you arranged her nightclothes on her bed in an order that was like a sign I could not decipher, a configuration that said, from now on, she would sleep differently.

TWO

We are killing time in a hotel bar. We are mutilating an hour, waiting for Anna's appointment with the cerebrovascular neurosurgeon who Dr. Mead has arranged for us to see at St. Michael's Hospital. Why time must always be so brutally disposed of in such circumstances, I do not know.

"Would you like vodka?" I ask Anna. She scans the drinks menu, but I know she will have one of two things: wine or vodka. Occasionally a gin and tonic, but it isn't warm enough for gin today. It isn't warm enough for anything today, even though we have passed the solstice and summer has been officially declared. I crave the return of my childhood summers: the consistent, reliable intensity of heat and sun that made living in this country bearable. Summers as a kid were longer than winters, only because so much happened in them; now they pass like a racing pack of wild things. Anna thrives in the heat, and I am getting too old for the cold that I was born into.

When you lay in the sweat-trough place we find every time, and you put your face in the pit of my arm and smelled me, I was ashamed and outdone by the quality in you that digs deeper than my desire will allow. "How do you feel?" you asked me. I was mute, shut down. And afraid that any answer would imprison me.

Anna chooses lemonade again and I'm surprised, but I shouldn't be. She is a woman who understands her body, and would not want alcohol to reduce her already diminished control. As for me, it's beer again. I gulp it down. It chills me more, and I rub my hands together to murder another minute.

"How do you feel, Anna?" Dr. Gottlieb asks when we finally get in to see him. It's the same, every appointment. I despise this trick question.

"I'm fine." Anna says nothing more.

I'm proud of her for throwing the trick back at him.

Dr. Gottlieb stares suspiciously, not understanding my wife the way I do—not knowing how powerful she is. Don't you see, doctor? She is the one in control. I find myself missing the insolent Dr. Mead, who, when Anna claimed her farm machinery identity, accepted her tease with a smile, as though he knew what game they would now be playing. Confabulators are not limited to, or inhibited by, their own awareness. Their brain has been set adrift in a galaxy of suppressed alternatives to their own consciousness. It's possible that the distinction between Anna's external and internal worlds is becoming vague. In our careful conversations at home yesterday, as we waited to confirm this appointment with Gottlieb, she said only one sentence, "Asparagus electrocuted the ravens," that caused me any alarm. I became convinced then that Anna is indeed playing with us, and is in complete control.

"The spies came out of the oven and were blue by the time I got to them, and when finally they opened their heads, the pyjamas were torn and all the furniture was wet," Anna says, unable to hold back any longer. Gottlieb's eyebrows slide up. My heart silently splinters.

He slowly checks charts and reports, the accumulation of the past weeks of testing. We wait for a pronouncement, but what I really want to do is pick up and leave, I want to take Anna home, and I don't mean to our house south of Stayner, where the corn has already begun to climb towards my waist from all this rain. I mean to take her to Istanbul, where we will both be warm and where the sun will order her words, as bud to blossom to fruit, in the natural order of spring to summer, not this mad weather, this mad language. As I shift in my chair, I can feel the edge of the sketch pad in my jacket pocket, and the point of the Staedtler liner protruding from it.

"There is an operation," Dr. Gottlieb offers, as though giving into something he hadn't really wanted to admit. Anna's eyes narrow.

"Doctor, please let us know everything," I say, but what I want to do is punch his nose flat into his face.

"It's complicated. It involves opening up the skull and fixing a clip on the artery. It's unlikely the flow will stop on its own, and more likely, if we don't do anything, the aneurysm will burst. Which would be fatal," he says, and looks out the window. "We can't take a chance. It's not like a leaky tap you can let drip."

I want to tell him he's the dripping faucet—this dripping bloody medical profession and all they think they know. I want to tell him to leave my wife alone and let her deal with it, because that's what she's always done, always managed—managed both of us, really.

"But the risk is high, you see," he continues, and again: all that we never know is coming. "There's a very high risk of brain damage, or even complete disability. And as with any operation, there is the risk of fatality . . ." He does that doctor thing and looks down at the chart as he says this.

Fatal is what life is in any case, I want to holler back at him.

We listen to some more details, and Anna rubs her hands together. I watch her fingers curl slowly over her knuckles. It is here, now, I think, that my marriage to this woman truly begins. Until now it has mostly been the "better" part of the deal. Here we go, sliding into "worse."

I cannot see any difference in her. Her skin is still beautiful, despite the age spots, those freckles of experience that dot her fawn-coloured complexion. She has only a few wrinkles beneath her dark eyes, and two lines that put her mouth in parentheses. Her lips have not lost any of their fullness, any of their moisture. She will be fifty-nine in September. This is a woman I have known since her late twenties, and this woman, I believe, right here, right now, in the shadowless sterility of Dr. Gottlieb's office, I love more than I did three decades ago.

I had been thinking of green, of the greens that I had seen in Indonesia a few months before I met her.

The green of a banana palm is fearless—a green that says it will endure, despite what those who live alongside it will do, despite famine, war, and the swarming of insects. This green says, ha ha, I am serpentine, and light is in my blood. Anna's shirt that night we met was the colour of those palms. She was nearly twenty-eight, doing a Master's in Literature at the university. I had just started DesignAge with my partner, Harry, who knew how things worked, who knew how to get himself a BMW and women, and who knew that we didn't have much time to make it; our time was now. Growing up I had believed that I would be a real artist, a painter, but necessity dictated something else, and I had become a prisoner to shapes and signs and the shared meaning they take on.

On a double date that Harry had arranged with his girlfriend Susan, the four of us sat at a long communal table in a bar. I was beside Harry and across from Anna. A man in a white shirt sat next to me, angled towards his girlfriend, who looked to be having a miserable time.

"Mike, you're not eating," Harry said to me, noting how I'd drifted off, though he might not have guessed that my thoughts involved the colour green. I clipped a french fry between my fingers and bit into it. It was cold, but I picked up another quickly on its trail and nibbled at it distractedly. I couldn't help wondering if Anna was a Muslim, as I'd learned on my holiday in Java that green had been Mohammed's favourite colour. The fact was that Anna's origins puzzled me. Her first name was ordinary, for a Canadian or a Brit or a Spaniard, a Columbian, a Czech. A small, ordinary name for a face so exceptional, and it threw me for the first hour of our dinner together. Harry had told me about Susan's fellow student, Anna, but he hadn't mentioned a surname, and it had felt impolite to ask upon meeting her. Her skin glistened like a mineral. As I watched her face it was as if different parts of the world rose up through it—the shiny, mottled variance of the earth. Look, there was south China or Malaysia, look again, the west coast of Africa, then Delhi, Persia, Lisbon, and suddenly somewhere Celtic.

"I can't believe you ate that," Anna said to me, smiling, revealing beautifully white teeth, slightly crowded in front at the bottom. The smile made the words a tease.

"Why not?" I asked, already powerless.

"They're his," she said, pointing to the bowl of french fries and then the stranger beside me.

I sat up straight, embarrassed, and she laughed.

"I won't tell anyone," she said, "and you do the same for me some day."

I would do anything she ever asked of me.

When I took her out the following week to the repertory cinema on Bloor, I was still too shy to quiz her about the continents in her face—the which, where-from and how of someone I thought was the most beautiful woman I'd ever met. Her beauty was not traditional, and that made it all the more powerful. She had bold, not refined, features—and her eyes were the quickest I'd ever seen.

"Can I help?" she asked a man in the street outside the cinema as we stood in a line with others waiting to buy tickets. I was confused as to why she was approaching this stranger with her elbow out towards him. The man took her arm; I pinged with jealousy. A minute or so later I realized the man was blind and that Anna was helping him navigate the crowd, which was making his passage along the sidewalk difficult. Anna had noticed his effort before I'd seen a thing.

During the film she kept herself tight in her chair. I have no idea what we watched, and was oblivious to anything but her.

We would lie in bed too long, exhausted by the night of Fred's wailing. We'd trace the rising stench to Fred's full diaper, but would try to ignore it, try to clutch the arm of a dream, to stay clear of duty before the sun rose . . . then one of us would laugh and we'd be bound by the shared trap of our existence.

Anna rarely talked about those early days between us—or about anything in her childhood, for that matter—as though memories embarrassed her. "I don't miss it. I was a baby when we left," she said to me after we'd been together a couple of years and I asked her why she disliked it when her parents talked incessantly about Istanbul, or when people asked her about her background. Her voice became sharp. "You think there's a more exciting place called the past, where they do things better, where they live with more flair. It's not true."

Her family was like a prism of loss: her mother wrote long, nostalgic letters to her friends in Istanbul; her father never learned English properly and didn't care to; her brother escaped the weight of their longing by reinventing himself as an American.

"Kiss me," Anna would say whenever I asked her if she wanted to make a trip back to Turkey.

But it is I who would like to travel there, back in time to the Istanbul of Atatürk, where Anna's father was born the year the office of the Ottoman Sultanate was abolished and an emboldened, hopeful republic established. I want to interrogate Anna's grandmother to learn the grace of her dervish heritage, to see her perform the whirl—forbidden to females—in the intimacy of her home, where, Anna's mother told me, she was renowned for out-whirling even the fittest of men. I want to watch her spin and to assemble my humility before her.

The past is punishing Anna for unrequited love, in-flicting itself randomly, then enlisting the present and future and conflating them all to torment her. And this feeling has not been as alive in me for over a decade as it is right now: this urge to take her, here, in front of our good neurosurgeon. I'd unbutton her palm-green blouse slowly—perhaps with my teeth—and release her overripe breasts and take one, the left one, in my mouth, to feel the nipple pucker on my tongue. The urge grows complicated at the thought of entering her, though. My first instinct is to move hungrily—she likes a gentle ride, but she can also be desperate to be subdued roughly, with a smack on her ass to make her skin smile. But this new marriage, just begun, this "worse" part of the deal, makes me hesitate about a playful fuck. Oh, but I would plant myself deeply in her, stay there, forever, let the surgeon separate us if need be. But why would that need be?

"I'll drive up tomorrow," Sasha says on the phone when I call her from home later in the day.

"No need, not so soon; she's fine," I mumble.

"She's going to have her head cut open!" she shouts to challenge my *fine*.

"She hasn't agreed to it yet . . ."

"Of course she hasn't; she's terrified. I'll see you tomorrow; I'm staying the weekend," and she hangs up.

I realize my daughter is saying that she's going to get a sub for her part in the chorus of *Dirty Dancing*, which she has been in for almost two years at the Royal Alex. This gesture is quintessential Sasha. The girl who has lived to dance from the age of four always knows her priorities. She stands out among the other dancers in the chorus because she is the least ambitious; she stands out because her hunger doesn't interfere with her delight.

I take an hour or so before I call the other two. Sasha will have already called to fill them in, with a gentle clarity I could never manage. When Fred finally calls me back after I leave a message on his pager, his encumbered voice promptly sets me to sketch a graphic to represent him.

"Dad, have they mentioned the possibility of embolization?" Fred asks. His voice strains as though I've scolded him. I must have scolded Fred too much as a child.

Charlotte doesn't answer her phone, but her voice mail clicks in: "Leave me a message; I don't read minds!"

Charlotte is stone, and yet I believe there's something flammable beneath the surface. Perhaps her sign should come with a warning. I leave a message as I stand in the hallway outside what was once her bedroom, where her trophies for the debating team, chess team, and young entrepreneurs' club still line the shelves above her desk. I can still feel the determination that intimidated me even when she was a teenager.

"Please call me," is all I'm able to say.

When the five of us gather around the Sunday lunch prepared effortlessly by Anna, I feel such an enormous sense of relief that I am close to letting go of all concern. I slice a sliver of the rosemary-garlic lamb and notice how perfectly cooked the just-pink meat is.

"Rabbits, hundreds of them, bounded as the corn came down around them, and if you open up the pie then all the blue jays fly out and in them there are twenty-four, twenty-five, no, twenty-seven babies each year, and the winds will take them away, and if Mike says he wants that, then okay."

Sasha reaches over to lower my hand, which has shot up with the knife in it, as though she's afraid I intend to use it on someone. I look at her with annoyance, then at all of them.

Fred cuts his lamb as though slicing into an I-told-you-so pie. His grey eyes flicker with neither humility nor grace. And yet. His hands are gentle. My son is not physically strong; he has soft hands and a soft face, but there is steel in his soul. When he was eleven years old, he told me that the best thing in the world was playing Civilization, when the barbarians invaded and took on his Mongolian villagers, battling in hand-to-hand combat, eventually losing to Genghis Khan, or when he was awarded gunpowder as he moved up the levels and used it to expand his empire. "Pa paaaaa!" he said, mimicking the computer game's sounds, "the greatest feeling."

Anna pushes her chair back from the table and crosses her arms. She smiles, knowing we are watching her, and says, "Eat up, then," and I wonder what she means by "eat" and what she means by "then," and if she really is saying "Fuck off, now." I watch her cross her legs and begin to shake her foot up and down, and then in little sideways movements, then sideways and circling. It's something she does—a nervous tic. Five years into our marriage that foot became irksome; the shaking felt like the rattlings of a mad woman. It contained within it all that Anna never said to me, even though she claimed to talk about her feelings so easily and had asked me to talk about mine. How I despised that foot and its compulsive, constant motion.

You hit me, there in the street, because I didn't know why women always had so many questions I had to answer.

As I stare at the pale heel that gapes from the sole of her sandal, I notice a callus, scaly and hard like a boat-hull barnacle, protruding from her big toe. I consider kneeling to lick it moist and soft, beg it to whisper my name and recount to me the days after the Bloor cinema, to give it all a date, a title, a proper heading in Anna's life accounting.

"Mom, we need to know what you want to do about all of this." As usual, Charlotte cuts through to what everyone else cannot express.

"Charlie," Sasha says, "I think she's just told us." What has Sasha understood from Anna that the rest of us have failed to grasp? How does she know?

"Look, I'm sorry everyone, to be like this again, but get real. If we don't do something there's a chance her brain will burst open like a water balloon. You want to watch that?" Charlotte says.

Anna's foot stops circling the air. My lips part, but I only lick them and stay quiet.

"Charlotte," Fred says, "You're a complete bitch."

"Fred!" I shout, and for the first time in years I am the disciplining father again.

"Mom, I want to play you the music from the show at Toronto Dance, and, oh, I have some photos. We start rehearsals soon, so I'm quitting this run of *Dirty*." Sasha announces a significant event in her life—and changes the subject—with an insouciance that neither of her siblings would ever be able to manage.

As Sasha stands up, her ribcage moves like a purl stitch that Anna once showed me as she was knitting a sweater for Fred. I gasp, and I see that the others have also traced the perfect, fluid line. Fred has taken hold of his left wrist. Anna reaches for Sasha's hand, and I realize that it's been a long time—two, maybe three years—since my wife has worn her wedding ring. Why do I only now consider the significance of that?

I didn't know the blondeness would make me want it again and again. I thought it would be just once.

"Dad, let's go outside. We need to talk," Fred says and I nod.

Charlotte looks at me as though this is all my fault. "Fred, in a second. First," she says, intercepting us and pointing with her chin in the direction of the kitchen, indicating to her brother that she'd like a private word with him. She looks at me with scorn.

"Dad, give me two secs. I'll meet you on the porch," my son says, accommodating us both. The two of them get up to conspire, and I push my chair back and head outside.

After our first date, and the foreign film that I will never be able to remember, I lost all capacity for sleep. I would work long days at DesignAge's trendy office on Queen Street West. I was prolific, and my design for a large optical chain, with an outline of spectacles buried in the firm's name, became my first major coup. Suddenly I felt like a man who could not fail at anything. For the entire eighteen months before we were married, I was high on my own brilliance. Anna's presence in my life seemed to confirm it, and that must have been why I asked her to marry me— because I wanted to secure the feeling for eternity.

Anna saw through me. I know now, decades on, that she was aware of every false move, every manic, gonad-driven step I took and didn't take, and yet she never let on that she could detect the slippery eel of fear inside me.

"How's your love life?" she asked me one evening over the red-checkered tablecloth at Fran's on College Street—a cheap night out because I was saving for a car. I looked up from my roasted chicken and chips. Her face betrayed nothing ironic, no hint of a trick.

"It's good," I said, stupidly.

"Why's that?" she asked, still looking serious.

"Because you're in it," I replied, treading lightly.

"I'm in it," she repeated back at me.

I looked at the prunish green peas on my plate, then up at her with a weak grin. "For good?"

Her eyebrows twitched towards one another. She raised her fork, piled high with the starchy pith of her baked potato, and took a mouthful. Doubt rattled through a chink in our familiar silence. I watched her, from under my lashes, as I cut into the chicken breast on my plate and, as I waited for her to say something, took a bite. Our chewing and swallowing was interminable.

"There was this couple today, on the subway," she began, finally, then paused to take a sip of her wine, "and the man was talking, about his work—he was some kind of marketing trainee guy—and he kept saying, 'so, as far as I'm concerned,' blah, blah, blah . . . before every point, 'as far as I'm concerned,' and he just kept talking and talking, and looking at her for a reaction and then just talking at her, almost like he was trying to convince her of something. But he was just telling her about his day: the man he was working with had been sick and he'd taken over his accounts. Nothing that required convincing. The woman—she was very beautiful. And pouty. Around my age, I think, or maybe a little younger. She just looked straight ahead and nodded, while he nattered on and on at her. I watched him talk until it was like he slowly ran out of gas, and the talk went sluggish, and sputtered, because when he looked at her maybe he thought she wasn't listening, so finally he just shut down. They sat staring forward for a little while, and then she looked at him, put her head on his shoulder, and started picking at a button on his jacket. Then she started talking. It was like she was taking up the baton he had dropped. She was off: telling him about her day, looking at him like she was begging him to pat her on the head or something. He just stared ahead, not even nodding. Just blinking now and then." Anna took another sip of wine and then another forkful of baked potato.

I was all too familiar with the scene she'd described, that subtle dance of abandonment that couples go through, when one leads and distances, while the other begs like a dog for scraps of attention, and then the positions reverse. I picked up one of the peas, now cold and even more shrivelled, and gently squeezed it without bursting the skin.

"Marry me," I said, looking up at her.

Her eyebrows did that twitch again, but then she smiled.

"You're something else," she said.

I had to ask her again, several times, before she agreed. When she told me that story about the couple in the subway, I took it to mean that we weren't like them—that things were right and balanced between us and that we didn't do the abandonment dance. But now I wonder if I got it all wrong, if maybe what she meant was that I should be more like that guy, and the story had more to do with my not talking to her enough, or not using my words with enough authority—*as far as I'm concerned.*

Maybe I wasn't giving her the pleasure she could have had from a more talkative man. Perhaps it was only me who was comfortable with silence.

"I've found a job," she said casually one evening when she'd come to my apartment with a bottle of wine and some blueberries, her favourite. Instead of excitement, I detected a note of resignation. That this is what people do: they graduate, they get a job, and they come home with blueberries.

"Hey, great! Where?" I stood up from my desk.

"George Brown," she said, then turned on the tap and ran water over the fruit. George Brown College had been her first choice out of all the colleges she had applied to, and the first one to respond to her unsolicited letters asking about possible positions for teaching English.

"Two courses, five groups, so that's twenty hours a week," she said, and I wondered if that was a good thing or a bad thing.

"Is that a good thing or a bad thing?" I asked.

She put the blueberries in a bowl and swept her long hair behind her ear and over her shoulder. She walked towards the table; I met her there and we both pulled out chairs. I kept my eyes on her.

"Those who can't . . . teach . . ." she said and took a handful of berries.

I shifted in my chair. "But you can."

"Can what?"

"Whatever you want."

Her smile was clenched as she shook her head.

"Do you want children?" she asked after a short silence.

"I don't know," I said, feeling ambushed. Why was she asking me that now?

Much later, I would prod her about her decision to teach. There were things she knew deeply—things to do with literature, politics, food, the directions to my brother David's cottage on Georgian Bay. There was her own Turkish history, her status as an immigrant, as one of untold millions who, like her family, had contorted their identities to become North Americans. Yet she chose to limit herself to paragraph construction, apostrophes and the proper use of commas.

Soon after she started teaching, I overheard her talking to Susan in the kitchen of our first apartment: "My mother never admitted she wanted more, but she never seemed satisfied. If she'd been allowed to, she'd probably have run a state, let alone a business, as well as bring us up, but you can't have it all. I won't be like her. I won't."

Her voice had been so determined that I had stepped back and returned to the living room.

Anna's father had been a teacher, greatly respected by the expats with whom he drank coffee at the local Turkish café on Dundas Street. Her mother had wanted to be a dancer—a dervish like her own mother, perhaps because it was forbidden—but in Toronto she had helped her husband to run a shop while raising Anna and her brother. Anna told me that her mother had often stared into space, a look that told Anna she was imagining the life she could—but didn't—have, thanks to the burden of a husband and children, and the Canadianness they were all meant to be learning.

Her parents died within two years of one another, both from cancer. These parents—the brainy Fatih and the dainty Lale—had been intertwined with our lives, excellent grandparents and babysitters to our children, keen gardeners, and players of bridge and other tabletop games. While Anna showed her parents a quiet respect, she seemed to view their lives as unremarkable, and very rarely spoke of the accomplishment of their reluctant integration into a new culture, or the simple happiness that existed between them. Her brother Joseph—Joe—had moved to Miami in his twenties and had last made an appearance at their mother's funeral, a decade ago. Before the service, brother and sister had argued on the same steps of the funeral chapel in suburban Etobicoke where, many years before, Fatih and Lale had stood with a sense of dutiful relief, having just signed the monthly instalment plan that would ensure that their own funeral services and interment were no burden on their children.

"You think you're special?" Anna had managed to choke out through tears. "You're not special. You're just like the rest of us, and when you figure that out, let me know." She turned away from her brother and composed herself by smoothing down the cropped black suit jacket that gathered at the waist to accentuate her slim figure. Carefully picking her way up the remaining stairs in her delicate-heeled shoes, she walked with dignity into the chapel. Her hair was now cut to just below her chin, but the life-long habit of swinging it over her shoulders and pinning it behind her ear was still a tic, like the itching of a phantom limb. When I asked her, later, what had happened between her and Joe, she shook her head and brushed the air with her long thin fingers to dismiss the question, but then she began to cry. She buried her head in my shoulder, sobbing, saying, only, "my mom."

When our children were growing up, Anna didn't dramatize her family for them the way I did, telling my grandfather's stories, recounting traditions and farmers' superstitions. It wasn't as though she was embarrassed about who she was or where she came from; it was more that her family was then, and our family was now. This was her accomplishment—a single-mindedness of purpose that has by association shaped my life. I resented her for it for many years. And yet, all along, it has also been that humility that I am fatally attracted to.

By the time she finally agreed to marry me—"Okay," she said, a tear sliding from the outer corner of her eye towards her ear, her breath hot, chest heaving, her sex still spasming, holding me inside her—I felt disarmed. From that day on, I believed that one day Anna would out me, and I would be seen for the fraud I was, and she, she would . . . what? Rule the world, no doubt. I'd let her, I'd decided, and would be content that if I had to lose her I would lose her to her own, bashful power. I still can make no sense of why that hasn't happened.

"Did you know that, Dad?" Fred says, touching my shoulder. I look up and realize he has been standing there without my noticing. "You didn't hear me. Never mind. I'll call you with the details later." What details? I have been far away, staring out at the horizon, not hearing a word he has said. He returns inside.

The day is overcast and the air sticky; finally some of the summer heat is arriving. I raise my hand to my neck and squash at least three blackflies with my fingers, wiping them off my skin. There's a hum that is much bigger than insects, but I can't trace it. Sasha comes onto the porch, and I look down at her as she stands beside me, gazing out towards the asparagus ferns as though she's spotted something. I notice she's holding a digital camera the size of a business card. I look over to where she is gazing, but don't see anything particularly scenic, then my eyes return to the camera. Suddenly I am struck by its size, and I try to decipher how it can hold my image, or hers, or that of the landscape before us. How are such things possible? For the first time in years, I am in awe.

"What's that sound?" I ask, now more bothered by the humming noise from out in the field.

"They're fertilizing," Sasha says, as she slips the camera into the back pocket of her jeans. She looks up at me. "Look, Dad, I think Mom wants to talk to all of us. We just have to let her take the time she needs." She holds the top of my arm as if about to squeeze my bicep, the way she did when she was a child, but she and I both know how my flexing now would fail that habit of love. I look at her face and think of pickles. Sasha suffered with terrible acne as a teen and a few scars remain. Her eyes are pale green like blanched cucumbers. She is not beautiful, not the way Charlotte is, but she is so much more attractive. Her face is concerned and yet confident. Nothing daunts her.

"I catch her sometimes," I start, thinking it's only to Sasha that I might be able to say these things, "watching her reflection in a glass window or public mirror, and she'll do a kind of 'Boo!' and pull a face, as though the real her had caught her physical self off guard, as though she knows it's all a joke."

"Everyone does that, Dad, don't you?"

There's a misshapen silence between us. I rerun Anna's "and you do the same for me one day" from the night we met. My guilt sickens me.

"Charlotte's leaving, and I think Fred is too. Dad . . . Charlotte said something a minute ago," Sasha begins, but then breaks off. Her eyes are glassy. "Is there something she's angry with you about? 'He won't stay alone long,' she said." Sasha sneaks a look behind her toward the kitchen, to make sure she's clearly out of earshot. I hear the muffled sound of Anna and my distant daughter laughing.

It's Charlotte I've disappointed the most.

"Sometimes, when she feels most strongly, she has to lash out," I say to Sasha, and I realize that I have invented this version of Charlotte and that in fact I know nothing about her at all.

"Let's go in," I say, wiping more blackflies off my neck.

When I return to the table and sit down, Anna and Fred emerge from the kitchen and sit with me. Sasha pulls out a chair and we wait, silently, for Charlotte to join us, but when that wait feels too long, Fred asks Anna if she has made up her mind.

"It's important to act quickly," he adds. "There's no time to waste, and even so, if you tell them now, there'll be a waiting period. Scheduling, tests, preparation, pre-op stuff . . ."

"I know," Anna says clearly and forcefully. "And if the buckets are filled . . ." She hesitates, and I hold my breath, "the farmers in the park become sugar for the king. You mustn't hobble them up in the rickets and make wretches of them. It's the law, and when riches sway and the moon makes its choice, well then, feet will rock, lemons will fall—"

"Mom, it's your decision, and your time," Sasha says abruptly, a horrified look on her face, corking the flood of her mother's nonsense.

"Sasha, please, cut the airy-fairy crap," Fred cuts in.

Charlotte enters then and stands behind Fred. The two of them seem to breathe in as one, positioning themselves as their mother's sentinels.

"Remember, Mom, this thing will get worse, not better," Charlotte says, and shifts the weight on her feet.

"And the technology these days . . ." Fred adds.

"We have a stake in it, too—"

"Charlotte, you selfish bitch!"

"Sash, please," Fred says. "If you recall—"

"I CAN REMEMBER THE FIRST WAS TREES!" Anna's raised voice cuts Fred off. "If the storm was France's creamy hotel, it would not smell like this. Don't you see the smell, the way it makes everything cold?" She stops herself, then looks at her fingers collected together obediently on the table. "I remember," she says, her voice now barely audible, but still insistent.

Charlotte glares in my direction, as if Anna's two keenly whispered words support her accusations against me. Charlotte is the one who most resembles her mother.

"Dad," Fred mumbles, and begins to walk towards the kitchen.

I push my chair back and follow my son.

"I spoke to Dr. Mead," he says, in a hush like a cop-show coroner. "Jargon aphasia is what it's called. It's semantic jargon, but not yet neologistic or even phonemic." He nods like one of those toy puppies in the rear window of cars whose necks are suspended on springs.

I have no reply.

As the blonde Tuesday turned into three months of Tuesdays, I watched my stomach flatten, my arms tighten; I felt my senses return to their peak.

"It means it's not just confabulations, but something associated with aphasia—the temporal gyrus or the posterior parietal operculum ... it means that it's possible there's more pressure than Gottlieb can fix."

It's not that I don't want to speak. I do. But I can think of absolutely nothing to say.

Charlotte comes into the kitchen and pats Fred on the shoulder as a signal that they should leave. Another thing that my daughter blames me for is the drive back to the city. If I hadn't insisted we needed a simpler, back-to-nature life, just at the time when Charlotte was needing a more complicated, teenage one, she'd be travelling a few blocks instead of an hour down Highway 400. She's right to blame me. I was the only one who needed this return to the expanses of corn that dominated my childhood. As I look out the kitchen window, I see that the stalks have grown even since yesterday.

When they have all gone, Anna and I sit in the living room in front of the evening TV—our choices being the home video shows filled with doggy mishaps and baby surprises, or the perpetually dismal news magazine shows.

"Leave this," Anna says when I choose *America's Funniest Home Videos,* and I revel in her clarity. "It's hard," she says after a few minutes.

"Yes," I say, alert to her every jitter, her flapping baby finger, her twitching foot. Maybe with these few, controlled utterances she is telling me that this is the way she needs to talk to me now: simple constructions, a few syllables at a time. So I take her up on it and decide to do the same:

"Can I get you something?"

"No."

"How do you feel?" God, I'm as bad as the doctors.

"Frightened."

I inhale.

"Would you rather be somewhere else?" And then I realize it's not a clear enough question. What I want to ask is if we should risk leaving, if I should take her to the mountains, which she loves, or do something that will get our minds off all of this, but of course there is no getting her mind off all of this. Her mind *is* all of this. "I mean, is there anything you'd like to do, to help this all be easier?"

"The baby will need changing and then there's all the clouds, and the dam on the highway that will only get worse," she says and I see that I've asked the wrong thing again. I hold my breath.

"What about the baby?" she asks me.

"What baby?"

"The one in the corn."

I don't ask her what she means. It's my job to know. I am her husband.

I wait.

But then my doubt and guilt grab me by the collar and I think I might choke. I wonder if Anna is finally confronting me, and I think that I now must face losing her.

"What baby in the corn?"

"Yesterday's," she says softly, in a tone that seems forgiving. I feel the urge to lay my head on her lap. I must be very tired. None of us has slept much this last week.

"Are you tired, Anna?"

"No, no," she says and smiles. She stands up and holds out her hand, beckoning me to join her. I take her hand, stand, and she leads me out of the house into the backyard that looks out on the field we've given over to the horses owned by the farmer next door. The night is warm and the punishment of the recent rainy days seems to have let up.

"Smell it," she says as she drops my hand, steps forward and looks up to the stars. I am beginning to see a beauty at work in Anna's brain. I toss my head back and smell and see and even lick the air, which tastes candied. Anna turns and steps back toward me. She puts her head on my shoulder. I wrap my arms around her and we breathe in tandem. I dare not ruin this by telling her all that needs to be said.

When Charlotte was eight and wanted to ride horses, you pretended it didn't frighten you; you pretended for her sake that you didn't know that a beast as powerful as a horse did not need to take commands from a tiny, if agile child who wanted the world at her feet. You told her that the horse needed her to tell it where it should take its wild energy. Charlotte blamed me when she finally did fall, years later, because I hadn't allowed her to ride the horse of her choice, the biggest one, the one with the blackest mane.

Later, when I am beside Anna in bed, her calf touching my shin as we spoon, I feel her breath quickening. Its rhythm reignites the urge I felt in Gottlieb's office. I touch her back, but worry that the force of this impulse to love-making will frighten her. I stroke her very gently. I feel our lust take its shape between our bodies, a memory becoming physical again. But then I think I hear something in her breathing. A rattle. I stop my stroking and raise myself up on my arm to look at her. Her eyes are closed, she is waiting, hoping, wishing, but I can't continue. I am afraid if I penetrate her that her head will explode.

THREE

"Is there anything else you want to know?" Gottlieb asks Anna, who is now out of the MRI tube. He has explained to us what surgery will entail for a brain aneurysm like hers. There's a chance that the confabulation will disappear within a few weeks, but there's also a chance that it won't. And even if it does, the aneurysm won't go away by itself. Clipping the balloon so that it doesn't get full to bursting is the wisest option, in Gottlieb's humble and oh-so-calm opinion. He lauded the appearance of the speech disorder as something that alerted us to the aneurysm that we can now monitor. Why is it that Gottlieb is so easy with these words—the who-knows-what of my wife's body?

Anna shakes her head: no, there's nothing else she wants to know.

"There's one last thing I would like to know," Gottlieb says.

Anna looks at him and waits.

"Why wouldn't you choose it?"

She stares blankly ahead.

"What could possibly make you want to live with the risk?"

I believe Dr. Gottlieb is now stepping—no leaping—over a line that should not be crossed. I sit up straight. If Anna doesn't belt him, I will.

"The first operation I had was to correct my knees; they were crooked at birth, and I had to wear callipers for years. The other children laughed at me," and here Anna's accent changes and instead of clear Canadian sounds, her speech becomes slippery with a tropical laziness, an accent that sounds South African or Australian. I've heard her imitate accents before—her mother's Turkish-inflected stammer, the Queen of England's posh pronouncements when she's in a silly mood, but this is not a joking matter and it feels as though the accent has her and not the other way around. "But I had to have the second operation in Marrakesh," she continues in the same thick tone, "and *thaayre thy* didn't *hayve* the right machinery, so my legs stayed crooked." This is not the open sluicing of previous confabulations; this is a body snatch. Anna has never been to Marrakesh, as far as I know, and her knees and legs are aligned and strong. I have seen her ski and remember her trying out Sasha's skateboard many years ago. No, this is someone else's life. "I had to take painkillers for seven years," she says, then mercifully stops.

Gottlieb looks at me, then back at Anna. "There's no reliable drug treatment for the kind of frontal lobe damage that is associated with this disorder," he says and turns back to me. "But there is an alternative method to deal with it."

She understands what you're saying, you moron; look at her, not at me.

"Endovascular coiling—it's not fully invasive. A platinum coil is inserted through the vascular system, into the head, and more coils are threaded through to block the blood flow into the aneurysm." He finally looks back at Anna. "Not all patients are equally suited to it. It depends on the position of the aneurysm. We need the results of this scan first."

"Doctor, what are you saying, exactly?" I ask, irritated.

"I'll have my colleague do more tests, Mike, and we'll see," he says flatly before turning to Anna again. "There are other patients you can talk to, assess the outcomes yourself."

Anna nods, indicating that she might like this, but then says, "I've spoken to the other patients; they don't know." She looks anxiously at me. "They haven't had the same window problems I have." As I pull the cuff of my shirt down over my wrist, I know she's not confused. She believes in these memories that have possessed her.

"We'll discuss it," I say to Dr. Gottlieb.

A few hours later, at home, Anna sits on our porch in the chair she chooses when she wants to be left alone. But I can't—I can't leave her alone. I get up from the kitchen table where I have been doodling, and I go, taking my marker and pad, and sit in the chair beside her. I look out to where she is looking, to the hills in the distance. Some days we see deer lying at the edge of the woods at the end of the road, but today we can't see much. The corn has grown more without my noticing, and it waves at me from beyond the driveway, as though chastening me for being unobservant.

There's so much I haven't told you yet, things I need language for. Like the time I ran away from my grandmother's calls, "Mike, Mike, Michael!" Into the corn. Four-month-old corn and eight-year-old me, corn that hid me, stalk and leaves like bodies making me one of their crowd, which minded me, didn't call me, allowed me and the wind to rustle it then pass, leaving it simply to grow.

"Anna," I say timidly. She looks at me, but her look says she's not ready to risk another conversation. But I need to tell her things—that one particular thing—and to have her know-it-all-ness pronounce upon me and damn me or forgive me. I want to be open, like she's always wanted me to be. Maybe like the man she dated before me, during her MA studies. What did I have to say back then about my feelings? Say that I feel itchy? Say that I feel unable to concentrate when you're asking me how I feel all the time? Say that I need space away from your questions? Because there's a problem I need to solve that has to do with objects in space, don't you see? Say what, exactly: that after three years of marriage, a toddler at home and you waddling pregnant through a suburban mall, that I didn't love the look of the ass on that woman who walked past us? Those were my feelings. Then. They are different now.

"I know you know what's happening," I say, and want to add, *and what has happened and what will happen*. She's so finely tuned to events and feelings that it's almost impossible to tell her anything; she's there miles before I am. I try to keep the conversation simple, and I am desperately trying to be honest. For once.

"But I need to know how you feel about all of this," I do add. I remember the couple in the subway, their dance of abandonment. "As far as I'm concerned," I try, but I don't know how to finish the sentence. Should I talk about my day? Should I shut up and hold back so that she'll talk to me?

"I feel locked out."

There. A feeling. A real, true and undeniable feeling. Surely she knows this, along with every small act of disloyalty that ever passed between us.

She looks over at me, her eyes wide open.

"Yes," she says. And then I wonder if she is telling me that I'm purposely locked out or merely conveying that she understands how I feel. "Three words," she says.

"What three words?"

"I can manage." And I want to take her by the neck and shake her. I know she can manage. She can manage the world if given the chance. And this is what I think now:

that she is always one step ahead of me. And yet she chose to teach; she chose to put her talents aside and teach. And in doing so she made me look even smaller for my ambitions. I want to tell her this.

"Three at once," she says, and I think I have them: I love you, I love you, don't you see that I love you? But this couldn't be what she means, not really.

"Please, Anna . . ."

"At a time."

"Three words at a time?"

"Yes. Otherwise, I . . ."

"I see."

"Help me, please."

And I will die doing so, I vow to her with my eyes.

I try to think of the questions, the right ones, posed just the right way. We are silent for several minutes while the corn grows.

"Do you feel like you have enough information from the doctor?"

"Yes, I do," she says.

"I want you to take your time to decide, but on the other hand it needs . . ." and I am about to blow it, I know.

"I have decided," she says.

"Good, good," I say, and wait. She will tell me.

"I want life," she says, and at first I am relieved, but then I wonder if she is saying she's not going to risk the operating table, because the chance for life is higher, in her estimation, if she doesn't go ahead with it.

"Does that mean that you will have the operation?"

"There are so many operations that I've had, especially in the navy, that it becomes difficult to tell the difference between them. You go down, you come up, it's all the same. And in Marrakesh—"

"ANNA!"

And she stops. I look down at her feet and see the dried skin and lines like cracked clay at the base of her heel. The hard callus that juts out at the curve of the bone looks as though it is expanding the big toe into a grotesque, witchy appendage with several black hairs sprouting from its skin. What has happened to her feet since the last time I saw this callus and wanted to lick it smooth? What is happening to me?

"I'm sorry," I say quietly. She looks back out towards the field. The sun is beginning to turn everything mauve, as though recognizing it has given off too much bright yellow light and must now soften.

When you were at home with the three of them, all still under the age of five, I stayed at work on purpose, trying to gain space. There was another one, not the blonde. A woman darker than you, fiercer, heavier, and so much freer than you. And I blamed you as we chatted over dinner even as you struggled with feeding and weaning. I blamed you.

I pick up my sketch pad and marker. I don't know it while I'm doing it, but I draw something for Anna. As I draw, I think about a woman. A dark woman with strong arms, who is picking up a heavy object shaped like a bucket that is almost twice her size. I think about her, but I do not draw her. Something else comes from my hands. This new kind of marking, like the one I want to make to capture the effect of Sasha. I think of the effort in the woman's brow, the sweat that marks her desire to give up. I think of all that I want to dispose of right now. When I've finished, I hold the drawing up in front of her and keep it there, waiting for her reaction.

She giggles and then laughs harder, holding a hand over her mouth, as though not wanting anything else to escape with the laughter. I think that perhaps she's making fun of me and that she knows something about what has inspired this drawing—the other woman, not the blonde, but the dark fiery woman all those years ago—but that's impossible. Perhaps she sees Marrakesh, toasters, callipers in there. This drawing is what is happening to us all now, and I think her laughter is some kind of acknowledgement.

I think I have found the way to talk to her in the present. The past takes too much language.

FOUR

"What time does she finish?" Charlotte asks with the re-hydrated contempt she's shown for me since we got the news. She clicks in her seatbelt. I start the engine.

I've picked her up in front of her office on Bay Street. My middle child works in a tower block, wears a power suit and works out at a gym every evening. My middle child dislikes being out in the sun for long periods for fear her naturally olive skin will darken even more. She has friends who own properties all around the world, while she struggles to pay the mortgage on a luxury lakefront condo she purchased two years ago, after Scott, her boy-friend of eight years, left her for his dental hygienist. My middle child is a cliché of a modern urban woman, and it's probably this fact, if I can admit it now, that keeps me at a distance. The truth is that her choices embarrass me.

"We'll have to be quick," I say as I glance over at her. She is not wearing her power suit today; she is in slim-fitting jeans and a T-shirt that show off her fine figure. "Why are you dressed like that?" My question sounds more accusatory than I intend, and if I were being honest I'd say it was a refreshing change to her usual angled and buttoned look. She doesn't answer as I pull out along Bay Street and get stopped at the traffic lights. We are meeting Fred in Yorkville for lunch. Sasha might be able to join us for dessert, once her rehearsal is finished. "They have casual Wednesdays too now in the corps, do they?" I try to joke, but she looks straight ahead at the road in front of us, and I think I detect a rolling of her eyes.

"Has she booked in for the op?" she asks.

"Yes," I say in defeat, and turn on the radio.

Anna is having another cerebral angiogram at St. Michael's to determine whether a coil embolization is possible, or whether the traditional and more invasive route of clip ligation surgery will be her only option.

"Thank God," Charlotte says, and throws her long chestnut hair over her shoulders, triumphant.

At lunch, Fred is generous, ordering a fine bottle of wine from our French waiter and telling me I'm looking well, when I know that my skin is sallow and caked like thirsty soil. He has on his doctor's demeanour—all confidence and impenetrability.

"Remember when Mom had to spend weeks in the hospital with Sash," he says, thus acknowledging that this particular grouping of the Williamson family is unusual. When Sasha was three years old, she developed pneumonia, with a fever that burned so high she glowed. Anna would not leave her side, slept beside her in the hospital, and we remaining three carried on without them as though we were a special unit in the family army, offering support to the front line by not drawing attention to ourselves, trying to reconstruct the feeling of Sasha without her there.

She was very ill for a month but recovered and has barely been sick a day since then.

"What are all of these words that Mom says?" Charlotte asks.

"Confabulation," Fred answers. "Damage to the anterior communicating artery, which affects the——"

"I know that much, Fred. I have been paying attention," she says, "but where does it come from?"

"We don't understand enough about false memories to explain why they happen," Fred says.

"She doesn't believe they're false," Charlotte says.

"That's right. For her they're real, true. She's right there in the moment with them as she's telling them." Fred lifts up his glass of merlot and stares into it as if through skin into blood.

"Maybe she's onto something," Charlotte says, and there's more than a hint of sarcasm in her voice.

"Charlotte, what is it?" I ask, my voice harsh.

"What is what?"

"What you need to say."

She looks down into her chèvre salad and a smirk plumps her lips.

"Go on."

"Nothing, Dad," she says as she takes a forkful of the cheese. As she's chewing, she looks up at me. "Maybe Mom doesn't want to remember things; maybe she's chosen other memories because hers are disappointing."

"Don't be an idiot," Fred says, piercing the last of his steak with his fork. He has eaten so quickly that I think this might be the first food he's had all day. But then Fred has never stood on ceremony with food or anything else.

"Dad? What do you think?" Charlotte asks. That sarcastic tone again. She is not too old for smacking, is what I think.

"Does anyone want coffee?" Fred asks, and it's clear he wants us to hurry up.

"Aren't you waiting for Sasha?" I ask.

"No, I have to get back."

Fred's residency in family medicine at Mount Sinai has been arduous. He is rarely available, his naturally curly hair has gone straight, looking like it has been cut with a bowl and clippers, and he looks twice his age of twenty-nine. I worry that he is bored with the lack of specialization, and I silently reproach him for not being ambitious enough to have pursued funding, for giving up once I pulled the financial plug.

"I have to get going too," Charlotte adds. "We don't have Sasha's boho schedule."

"Why are you so angry?" I shout, and I startle her into looking me straight in the eye. Her brow creases as though she will cry, and I see the little girl again.

"Dad," she says and, despite my very real animosity, I want to hold her. She says nothing more, and I wonder if she finds my need for her to be kind to me right now repulsive.

"I don't think she feels this like you're imagining," I say. "Dr. Mead said that confabulators believe what they're saying. She's not confused; she doesn't think she's making anything up. She just reacts to our faces looking confused, like we don't believe her."

"That's right," Fred confirms. "It's only because we look like we don't believe her that she has trouble."

"But she's so far away." Charlotte's voice is strained.

"No, no, she's not," I say, remembering the way the lust rose between us as I lay beside her, and I picture her face against her pillow—a face asking for all dreams to come true.

Anna had been closer to me then than she'd been in years.

"You like that she has the wrong memories," Charlotte says finally, and I feel the clawing of family spiders at our necks: the net-casting tricksters whose silky threads never let us forget for long just how strongly we are bound to one another. Finally I understand what Charlotte has been getting at.

"I'll ask for the bill," Fred says.

"And I'll meet you outside," Charlotte says, standing up.

"And I'm waiting for Sasha," I tell Fred.

But Sasha doesn't arrive before I need to leave to pick up Anna from the hospital. I find myself taking Charlotte's side about my daughter's bohemian schedule.

"You look beautiful," I say to Anna as I glance over at her in the passenger seat. The traffic has come to a halt as we turn onto the ramp for Highway 400 to head north. In the summer, even on weekdays, this highway is crammed with people headed to cottages or campsites.

She looks over at me, smiles and nods.

I took her skating once, at City Hall. She didn't know how to skate and held onto me for balance. I made a show of teaching her, and forced her to loosen her grip, as I checked around us to see if anyone was watching.

I notice that the hair at Anna's temple, and a swash of it from her forehead up along the part, is grey. Her roots are overtaking her monthly tint and I wonder if she has noticed and doesn't care about hair anymore, or about eyebrows or waxing, or her weight, which has stayed a perfect 135 pounds even after three children. She is toned for a woman her age, and up until a few weeks ago was cycling and swimming regularly.

She rushes, on the inside, my Anna. She surges with the force of a current—not water and not electric, but like air: the updraft that carries a wing.

The traffic begins to move again and we pick up speed. "Are you disappointed?" I say.

She looks at me with a furrowed brow that asks, *by what?*

And now I regret my question, but I have to follow through. I try to give her the question and answer together. "That the embolization can't be done in your case because of the position of the aneurysm."

"I'm disappointed that they didn't give the anaesthetic, though. It hurt a great deal, that operation, and when the goat knocked over the fence and the pole fell on me, it really stung, and so it would have helped if they'd given me the proper medication. They never do, though, this is what I've heard. The rain comes and the goats just trample over everything."

"Goats? How many?" I ask. The animals are back, and I don't know what gets into me—whether it is perversion or honest pleasure—but I want to follow her words. I want to be out there with her and her goats in the rain.

"Six or seven. They're cunning, but you know, so sweet, almost like dogs. The black fur barking digging dogs in Harewick."

"Harewick?"

"In Sussex—headless dogs."

"And the goats? Are they headless?"

"You're being silly," she says angrily and looks over at me. She thinks I'm playing with her damaged frontal lobe. "Make the cart less heavy and shuffle the wheels so it runs straight, with bright pink magnifying glasses. There's no poem for the poor old foot."

I nearly step on the brake, but there is too much traffic. I have to keep going. No animals, but she has said something that feels obscenely familiar. Then she's off again.

"The fleecing child came back. The one with the yellow hair and the slanted eyes. Do you remember her? She wanted to take our cake that day at the picnic. She was so thin. Her cold eating bones, her makeshift chariot. She brought the beans—it was her."

"Anna," I say to interrupt her, and to stop my dreadful feeling of shame for having started this.

"Wet, sarcastic hibiscus," she says, and when I glance over at her I see that she has three fingers up, having counted each of the words. Wet. Sarcastic. Hibiscus. Confident she has been successful, she peers out the window. I wonder if she's seeing something I should take note of.

The bubble in my wife's brain has put her in the very act of living rather than the ordering of it. Language is the action itself. I am desperate to be as alive as that. But I am a slave. Guilt—not gilt—chains. If I tell her, then maybe they'll drop away from me. If I tell her, there might only be us, together.

We finish the drive in silence and arrive home to the quiet of our land, which hums with insects and the reach-reach of the growing crops and the weeds that surround them. It's only five o'clock, and the endless July evening stretches out awkwardly before me. My desire to toy with Anna's mind is as strong as my wish to understand it, so it's best to avoid her.

I take a long, meandering walk through the asparagus field, now rid of its spurs and gone wild with tall, frolicking ferns. I find myself at the edge of the cornfield. I breathe in deeply. There's a smell to the stalks of corn that is erotic, but it's a childhood lust. I enter the field and walk along the rows carved out by the plough, in among the stalks that shove me side to side, nudging me to feel disgust, or sorrow, at all I have never become. But I resist their bullying and walk straight through, until I reach the other side.

I do not get lost.

I pick another row and do the same thing, walk straight through, and I think about what Dr. Mead told me when he gave us the original diagnosis. The aneurysm is only a symptom of something else. Some of its possible causes are brain tumour, trauma, a genetic disease that affects collagen, or polycystic kidney disease. These causes obviously range in degrees of seriousness, and will be tested for, but there was one other possible cause I haven't been able to shake from my thoughts, one that has haunted me: infectious material from the heart.

I leave the corn to its humming and return to the house. Resolved. Intent.

Upon removing my shoes in the hall entrance, I hear a whisper. Then an intake of breath less urgent than a gasp. The whirring of the washing machine in the final stages of the cycle muffles the sound. Our machine is modern, European-designed, and very, very fast; I follow its hum.

When I arrive at the laundry room door I stop just before I might come into view. I see her leg, her thigh, with her other leg curled over it in a squeeze, forming a crest at her sex. Her hand is cupped over the muff of hair there and it works in rhythm with the spin of the washer. Her legs tense and relax. Tense and relax. I step forward and peek around the doorframe into the room and gaze at Anna's face, as it concentrates on the spin, and reach-reaches . . . My wife is spinning inside. My lust rises, then stalls when I recognize how unnecessary I am just now. Her face tightens and her eyes roll back.

And there. Just there. My naked wife, with a lethal, peanut-sized swollen vessel in her brain dictating the entire history and future of her being, comes.

She comes to the hum of the washing machine.

I stumble forward, halfway to my knees, but quickly right myself and disappear to the kitchen with my shame.

FIVE

I am wrong to say Sasha was never sick again. There was another time, another visit to the hospital, but the circumstances were very different, and that time I was the one with the fever.

As I lie in the hot dark with Anna asleep beside me, a chorus of tree frogs breaching the dense blackness outside, I remember the events leading up to Egypt, a dozen years ago. Those last few moments of my innocence.

"What do you think of these?" Anna had asked me, enthusiastically, as she posed on the stairs. She was wearing a dress cut above the knees, and she twisted to show me the back of her calf and the thin seam of her romantically old-fashioned stockings. I felt my stomach lurch, but it wasn't a pleasant feeling.

"What are you doing?" I asked, and giggled nervously.

"I'm wearing stockings," she said, turning back to face me, her excitement now deflated. She stood with her arms at her sides, waiting to see if I would say more. I stared at her legs; though still slim, there was a sagging at the knees that I hadn't noticed before. She was turning forty-seven, and the dress she wore was the "little black dress" she had decided she needed to celebrate this birthday, "before it's too late."

She had become anxious about the idea of closing in on fifty, as though suddenly sensing her mortality. "Oh my God," she'd say when she noted friends and colleagues who were reaching the milestone that year. When Susan had turned fifty in July and Anna threw her a special party on our back lawn, my wife seemed to take on the half-century as if it were already her own. My job as host was to put steaks on the barbeque, and I was happy to have a specific task and not to have to engage in small talk about education cuts and increased class sizes. As I was tending to my duties, I overheard Anna make a flippant comment about old ladies, and I was touched and amused by the response she received from the teenaged Charlotte. "Mom, you still smell nice," she said. "Old ladies smell weird."

For the night of her birthday I'd suggested a dinner

out at Canoe, a chic restaurant on the fifty-fourth floor of the TD Bank tower, which Susan had recommended. Anna had made an effort with the black dress, which showed off not only her legs but exposed her arms as well. I tried not to notice the looseness of her triceps as she raised her arms to push her hair behind the ears.

"You look great," I said, hoping to restore her enthusiasm and recapture mine.

"It's a full moon," she said, and I knew that the confluence of moon and birthday was significant to her, that it meant something magical, which she wanted me to share in; but I was too tired for magic.

I desperately needed a holiday. Our children—18, 16 and 13—had filled our house with grunge and garage music, had insulted me too often with their that's-so-seventies-Dad opinions, and I was starting to feel undervalued at work. Undervalued and slowly withering. I had shone in the years of new standards in international pictograms, a craze that had begun with the Munich Olympics and continued through to Montreal 1976, for which I had perfected the curve of a man boxing, the distinction of a figure playing volleyball or badminton, and the angle of an alpine slalom. That craze had begun to subside. The standards for public information, culminating in ISO 7001, were being set in place. While I branched out and created designs for an ever wider variety of firms, my creativity was consumed by making a living.

On that evening in September, at the end of our extravagant meal, we looked out over the lights of the city. Anna had ordered oysters, foie gras and lobster, fully indulging in this treat. I could see our reflections in the window, surrounded by the vaguer figures of other diners. The scrambled light and the reflection of candle flickerings made me feel as if I was inside a malfunctioning kinetoscope, its sprockets entangled, images superimposed in error. I had to close my eyes against the soupy, disorienting panorama. We polished off a dessert of chocolate mousse and vanilla wafers and I sat, full, tired and silent over coffee, as Anna opened the gift I had bought with Susan's guidance. She took the gold necklace with the topaz pendant out of its delicate box and placed it around her neck, happy, I believed, that I had been tasteful in my choice.

She smiled up at me. "It's beautiful."

I was thrown by the bit of chocolate and wafer caught between her teeth. I noticed, too, the mascara, clogged like black sleep, in the tear duct of her right eye. I hurried us through the final rituals of our meal. I wanted to be home. Asleep.

As we got in the elevator to descend to the parking garage, I looked again at Anna's face. The black sleep was still there, and now, in the fluorescent lights of the confined space, I saw that the caking foundation makeup was doing the opposite of what it was intended for, highlighting instead of hiding the dry lines around her eyes and the splintered creases around her mouth.

"Happy birthday," I said, again. I'd repeated it too often by now, I knew.

In the full-moon drive home, Anna played a Cat Stevens CD, listening to it with a relish that irritated me.

That night in our bedroom, she came to me, still in her black dress, as I sat on the bed. I was in a movie. Her movie. She lifted up the dress and straddled me. I closed my eyes, desperately trying to summon the hard-on that would please her. As we made love, I kept my eyes closed, then turned away from her the moment we'd finished.

"Happy birthday," I said, and stayed tightly on my side.

The winter of that year turned bitterly cold, with long, bright days at minus 20 and below, which made my skin itch and increased my irritability. The sunshine was a lie, a trick, and the furnace roared with the rumbling depletion of my salary, thanks to the children who regularly left the front door gaping open in the absent-minded to-and-fro of their adolescent lives. I became desperate. I even went so far as to try to convince myself that time away, even accompanied by Anna, would help. I tried to talk her into a trip by saying that we needed to be on our own for a while. She had no interest in travelling, and told me, as she gathered up the lazily tossed clothes that littered our living room, that the children needed her more now than when they were young because their inner worlds were complicated. To which I loudly said, "BULLSHIT!"

She sat down and stared at me for some time before looking up to the ceiling where, presumably, she found the words she needed: "You are so selfish."

We had taken many trips as a family—to Western Canada, the American South, even the obligatory pilgrimage to Disneyland—but we had not been away on our own since the children were born. I had been to the Far East for business, but she had been unable to accompany me then because the children had been too young.

She had always complained about March, a cruel month with false springs and bitter winds that were like a payback for hope, so after she took her eyes from the ceiling I caught them, and pressed on. "We need it. Somewhere warm. What about Turkey?" For some reason I still needed her to want to return there, to want our children to know where she had come from.

And she did it again, just as she had for almost twenty years, since that first time in Fran's: the eyebrows twitching together and then that smile. I could have slapped her.

We spent a few days both trying to lead in the abandonment dance—that hardened two-step I eventually had grown so adept at. She watched television with the children after dinner, went to do her part-time teaching in the morning, and came home in the afternoons to attend to their so-called emotional needs. She cooked some meals, I cooked others. We went to bed. She read. I pretended to fall asleep immediately.

A couple of weeks like this and usually one of us would tire, needing to change up the moves. Anna returned one day from teaching and came to me in the kitchen.

"Egypt."

I looked up from the pot of beef stew I was preparing.

"I'd like to go to Egypt—see the Nile. The children have all done projects on it at one time or another. I know all about it, but I can't really imagine it."

I went back to my stirring and did not speak. But she stood beside me, waiting.

"I thought this wasn't a good time," I said, finally, taking the stew off the burner. I have never quite managed seamless humility.

"It's the perfect time. March, like you said. I'm sorry."

I was hers again, much too easily.

Her presence in Egypt seemed as natural as Nefertiti's.

Upon entering the first gate of the temple of Karnak, where the silt had been excavated to reveal graffiti from the kind of travellers I would like to have been—the Indiana Jones-type man who would have carved "Michael" into a pharaoh's obelisk—I began to feel that everything in my life had led me to this spot. The hieroglyphics—these beautifully carved translations of power—made me feel dizzily small. The temperature was a dry 32 degrees;

the sun bore down on my stubborn head, while Anna had wisely worn a wide-brimmed hat that shaded the burgeoning lines on her neck.

The Nile could have flooded and drowned us then, the pharaoh might have proclaimed higher taxes, the gods might have asked for greater human sacrifices, and I, gratefully, might have been spared the humiliation of my modernity.

"I am Mustafa," said our guide, and I felt something between him and Anna instantly. He was an average-looking man: glasses, black moustache, a soft, not muscular build. He shook our hands, and I noticed he held Anna's longer than mine. "Where are you from?" he asked her.

"Canada," she said, then realized from his look that this was not enough. "I was born in Istanbul."

He stared at her harder. "Of course, of course, I see. But I thought you were one of us!"

I needed to fuck my wife then more than I had in several years.

As the sun roasted my neck pink, Mustafa told us about the king who had died having left no sons to rule. His daughter, Hatshepsut, took the throne despite her sex and ruled Egypt with imagination and determination. Mustafa showed us where she was depicted in carvings and paintings as a male figure, and where her stepson later defiled her image. I felt Mustafa was talking only to Anna, so I retreated into the shadows to listen, while my wife politely nodded her head, again and again. She looked fascinated, and occasionally brushed her hands along the stone to touch what seemed like the manifestation of Mustafa's words.

He taught us how to read hieroglyphics, which I had once, long ago, studied. But there, in front of the Obelisk of Ramses II, I felt as though I was finally learning the craft I had been practising for more than twenty years. I knew the symbols for "make" and "life," and could just about make out the subtle prayers of the scribes for their king and queen or deity. But I had believed that a hiero- glyph existed more independently than Mustafa was suggesting. He taught us how to read ideograms and cartouches, to decipher the depictions of battles in the carvings by reading them like a story. I saw the inter- dependence, noticed how "make" and "life" were only part of a refined, intricate narrative, and the signs became truly meaningful for the first time.

"There, there, you see there." Mustafa pointed to a panel depicting a boat being carried by soldiers. "Some colour remains, beautiful colour."

I tried to read the other panels in front of me, but my memory of the alphabet was poor. Ankh and Horus's eye stood out consistently. I comforted myself with them as I strode before the artisans chronicled in the midst of their daily activities—weaving, making pottery, and the para- mount fetching of water. Kings were displayed with their enemies below them, and slaves on either side fanning them. Oxen were powerful and cherished. These signs were the yield, merge, and deer crossing warnings of their time. Yield to the King. Merge with the progress of civilization. Honour the beast of burden.

"But slaves . . . slaves," I muttered. "All of this built by slaves."

Mustafa stopped in his tracks and looked at me. He raised his forefinger and wagged it as though I'd blasphemed. "No," he said coldly. "Let me assure you: they were not slaves. That is a wrong impression. They were prisoners, captives from enemy nations, yes, but they were workers, paid for their work with food and homes. This is something you have wrong." Perhaps he, as an Egyptian, knew the truth. Who was I to say? But I couldn't get the idea of forced labour from my head.

"Look, look there, you see?" said Mustafa, pulling me away from a panel where I had been examining an image of an ox and cart, and pointing upward. "Hatshepsut and the god of fertility, you see, see there?" I looked to where he pointed, and he pulled me in closer. He rubbed his hand along the wall, and finally I saw what he wanted me to see: the god of fertility's erect penis was pointing straight at the female pharaoh, and through the sunlight and dust motes and shadow of stone, it was mocking me. "The god Min is often symbolized by an ox—a bull," Mustafa added and took out his solar laser pointer and shone it on a shaded panel above our heads. His pointer traced a beast in the field; next to it stood Min, brandishing a thunderbolt.

Later that day, on the west bank of the Nile—the bank of the setting sun, the bank of dusk and the twilight of life, where the Pharaohs built their tombs to wait out eternity—Mustafa took us to Hatshepsut's temple. He seemed obsessed with this female pharaoh. Built into the east face of the mountain that barricaded the Valley of the Kings from the Nile, the temple was the spot where I have felt the hottest in my life. Mustafa described, again mostly for Anna, how Hatshepsut built the temple here because she planned to link it with her tomb, which was being built, simultaneously, on the other side of the mountain. But the rock proved impossible to tunnel through, even for the Egyptians, and the mountain now stood forever between the female king and her temple. How disappointed she must have been upon her death, Mustafa said.

Anna smiled at him, knowingly, as I took a step back.

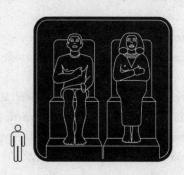

In our hotel that afternoon, as I rode Anna like Min rode his ox, I could not stop blathering about how much I loved her.

When we returned home after two weeks, we were tanned, relaxed and intimate. I held her hand on the plane. We smiled at the memory of what had gone on between us, in the hotel room and, particularly, in the desert tent. I felt I could, once more, be forever under this woman's spell.

We were met at the Toronto airport by Fred, with his hair cut shorter than it had ever been before. He seemed older than eighteen, like a man who had serious business on his mind. He was about to start university in the autumn and was already determined to go to medical school. He barely looked at us when we emerged through the sliding doors from Arrivals.

"There's some news," he said.

I felt Anna's body go rigid, as if all the ease the sun had given her had retracted, and in that instant we snapped back into atrophy.

In a bed in Cairo, the touch of your thigh on my cock transformed it. Midas fingers, Midas lips, Midas cunt.

Sasha had taken drugs and was in the hospital.

At her bedside in the emergency ward, seeing my daughter unconscious and gaunt, yet still more beautiful than when we'd left her, I knew that what I'd touched in Egypt was gone. "I'm staying here for the night," Anna said, and her voice pushed me into a back corridor of our marriage, where I would remain long after Sasha's recovery the next day.

Two weeks later, in the park behind the DesignAge office, the blonde hair would snag me; a cliché bait for a man whose whole life had been defined by his preference for dark hair, brown eyes, long legs. I was a man, who at the age of forty-nine, became the prisoner of a short, bosomy woman in her thirties with green eyes that made a laughingstock of emeralds.

SIX

I am skittish around the machines in the house—the dish-washer, the dryer, even the blender—anything that Anna focusses her attention on. My stomach clenches at the sound of an appliance, as though holding in something that is the last of all that is mine alone.

Even so, Anna seems less intent on the whir and spin of things than she is on building piles of objects around our house. There is a pile of letters, junk mail she has refused to throw out, on the kitchen counter beside the telephone. A pile of hats has grown on the floor of our bedroom near her dresser drawers. I hadn't considered how she might look after the operation, but clearly she has and is preparing for it.

The recovery time in hospital after the surgery is four to six days, the first days in intensive care. The home recovery period ranges from three to six weeks, "if the surgery isn't complicated." Doctors like Gottlieb must say these things to cover themselves against potential fuckups. Anna is obviously planning long into this recovery period and so must I.

A pile of novels is growing beside our bed. It's composed of authors I haven't known her to read before: Jane Austen, Herman Melville, and, oddly, Jack Kerouac—as though she's revisiting some thread of her MA studies that isn't yet apparent to me. If I weave that thread through the things she says, will I be able to decode what is going on in her head? Still, there are other piles that seem to have no significance to the past or to how she will spend her recovery time.

One I discovered yesterday, outside, at the back of the house where she normally has potted plants, gardening tools and bags of soil for her flower garden (which often fails in this sandy terrain). There a pile of cookware has grown: saucepans, griddles, frying pans, kettles, soup pots, a wok. I hadn't realized we owned so many pots, and when I went to the cupboard below the kitchen counter, I saw that all that was left in it was one small stainless steel saucepan that might be sufficient to boil an egg.

Another pile is growing in the living room next to the television. This consists of every lifestyle magazine and journal that has been brought into our home over the years as renovations, beautifying facelifts and spring cleaning were contemplated: *Architectural Digest, House and Garden, Redbook, Farm Beautiful.* A pile of suggestions for all that has never come true. There is a tall pile next to that one of *Maclean's, Harper's, Glamour* and *Modern Dance.* What for? There might be a pattern if I try to link these titles, or link the piles—magazines, pots, hats . . . There is yet another in the bathroom, which disturbs me most of all: a pile of items that must have been on the shelf for years, accumulated not only by Anna but also by our daughters. On the floor, near the toilet, the pile begins with a rubber contraceptive diaphragm stuffed with several individual packets of condoms to help keep its shape and firmness; three pink contraceptive pill dial dispensers rest against the dome of the diaphragm. On top of the dispensers are two pregnancy detection sticks, and on top of those are balanced two tubes of spermicide.

I want to understand the meaning she is building out of the detritus of our lives.

She is sitting on the porch again, in the Algonquin chair that I have thought makes her look like an old lady. She does not look old now; in fact, she looks younger today than she has in many years. It is I who am old; she has only grown old beside me, on account of me. But she has abandoned even that now and her eyes are as fresh as a teenager's.

I would come home late and lie, and act fatigued from work and take a shower; later in bed, I would take you to assuage my guilt, or argue with you to disable my conscience.

The day is cloudy, the air is close and almost adhesive. There are countless blackflies and mosquitoes, but she doesn't seem to mind, or even notice. If I stand behind her like this, for long enough, will her silhouette offer up an answer?

"Bugs aren't too much for you?" I ask, as I sit down in the Algonquin chair next to her. I hate these chairs. Why did we ever think they suited us and should adorn our porch? Why on earth do we have a porch? Why aren't we on a hot hilltop looking out over a raging sea? How could a porch ever represent the life we are meant to be living?

I swat away a deer fly.

"Mmm?" she asks, looking over at me. She hasn't heard or perhaps hasn't understood. It's not important.

"You've been clearing out, I see."

She nods, and I'm happy I've remembered the right way to talk to her.

"Things you don't need."

She nods again.

"And things you will."

Her third nod comes with a smile. We've both got the hang of this.

Kingfishers. Birds in the oak trees in front of the house titter and spring from one branch to the next and crows land in the corn field that edges the driveway. The world before us is flapping, gliding, and my head begins to spin.

"In the wintertime," she says, and the one, two, three of her fingers accompanies the words. She has control of them. She stops and breathes deeply, "the sea is," then three fingers on her other hand, "not so rocky," more breathing, one, two, three, "nausea not dizzy," she says. And something in this convinces me that she has heard my thoughts, knows what is going on inside me. I can never keep up with her.

She releases another deep breath, and with it: "This sea and the Baltic are different. I straddled the Baltic. It was summer. The crests of the waves were so high they knocked me over into the tiptoeing ships across the top like tiny pinafores—"

"Anna! Do you still love me?" I am shocked by myself. She looks over at me for a moment.

"Of course, yes," she says, sounding puzzled. I see the fingers in her lap fly up in succession. One. Two. Three.

"I'm sorry," I say. I want to take it back. I want to say instead, "What is love?" I want her to know about the tinny chiming in me that wants her to die, so that I no longer have to feel.

"There were crows out again," she says, and this is real. True. She places her forefinger over her lips as she gets up from the chair and stands in front of me. She crouches down and is on her knees and reaching for my feet. She grabs my running shoe at the heel and is pulling it off. My right foot is now bare, and she reaches for the other shoe. She takes my left foot in her hand and starts to massage it, beginning at the heel, moving up through the arch and finally to the base of my big toe.

Her name was Christine. An ordinary name, an ordinary woman I saw at least three times a week and melted into like an extraordinary man would.

As Anna massages my feet, I can see insects land on her neck, her arms. She doesn't flinch or take her hands away to swat at them. I cannot move to help her, but it could be now, here, that I tell her about the three years that it carried on, that blondeness and that sheer, blunt access to the tiniest parts of myself accessible through my cock. And perhaps it will be this revelation that will burst the bubble in my wife's brain. Disgust and love are similar, easily confused; they both burn up the heart and make you weak.

I lean over and take Anna's hands. I pull her towards me. She is on her knees between my legs, and I hold her shoulders and bring them tightly towards my belly. Her head rests on my chest.

"Please don't," I whisper.

"Don't worry, please," she whispers back.

"Let's go for a walk," I say and release her shoulders.

We both stand. I put my shoes back on. Anna heads towards the back field leading to the woods that line the river. I follow her like a man who has never known a single thing about life.

SEVEN

"You make a sound I've never heard before," Christine said once, having grown bolder with me after the first six months of coyness—her modesty overcome only during sex.

"What sound? When?" I adjusted my position and propped my head up on my hand.

"You know, just in that second . . . at the end." She turned to face me. We lay naked on her bed, which had a view of Rosedale Valley. She'd brought wine and set out outrageously priced snacks from a Yorkville deli on the sheets. "Do you share genes with, say, a cricket?" she said, giggling, which was infectious.

Giggling was something we did well. That and sex. And the dreaming—the what-ifs that filled our conversations over dinner.

"What if we woke up one day to find that there were no vegetables?"

"We'd be very upset."

"Some people would like it."

"Those some people would be under the age of five."

And we would giggle.

"What if I went in and quit tomorrow, hitchhiked to California to make it big?" Christine's parents had been born in Sweden, but the only Scandinavian thing about her was her looks—in other ways she was born to live in California. She was a clerk in a large insurance company, but she had a dream of becoming a singer. She always sang around her apartment, and although at first I had cringed at the thought that she imagined that at thirty-five she still could be discovered, I grew to like the songs, the notes she hit, the lyrics she knew flawlessly. She'd stop what she was doing and ask me to name a song, any song. I'd think hard, trying to make it difficult for her with "So Long, Marianne" or "Like a Hurricane" or anything that came to mind that I thought she wouldn't know or would never be able to sing. She'd pause for a moment then start, slowly, with an intro beat—I could see her counting in, two three four—and she'd sing, "Once I thought I saw you, in a crowded hazy bar . . ."

Things with Christine were in my control. She liked what I did, and was intrigued by my work. I showed her my drawings, talked about the business. She let me decide everything—the song, where to eat dinner, when to turn up, when to leave—and it was probably this, this simple, acquiescent arrangement, as my abs tightened and the love handles shrank, that kept me going back, until I realized we'd formed a team of some kind. Not exactly a partnership, but a duet. At home I would watch as Anna became more and more immersed in Charlotte's homework, Fred's university applications, Sasha's dance lessons.

And then, a year and a half in, Christine said, "What if I got pregnant?"

I was silent.

"I've stopped talking the pill."

My panic felt orange in colour.

"What if?" she said.

"Why would you?"

"It's what women do." Her answer was tinged with contempt.

"What about your singing?"

And I had become wretched now.

"You're never going to leave them, are you?"

I should have ended it in that moment, but the loyal man that I believed myself to be did not want to let her down. I didn't want her to think I wasn't the man she had fallen for. What if I could manage both lives? I would let things ride. I would keep everyone happy, I told myself.

"We can see about a baby," I muttered, and poured us both more wine. The fact that I had got away with something gave me new momentum. I began to tease myself with the new what ifs. Then and there I soldered the links of my new chains.

Charlotte had been on the debating team at her high school, already arguing at sixteen for free-market values. Her skills were most clearly employed in opposition to her parents. She was a stroppy teenager, but not a stereotype. She could turn on the charm, help about the house, and show compassion and generosity at one moment, then, wham, a door would slam, her temper flare and an argument erupt. She'd confront me on the restrictions I'd implement—no television on school nights, a curfew of eleven o'clock on the weekend—by planting herself in front of me and not moving. She was like a cowboy in a western, standing her ground, hands in her pockets as though poised over holsters. I usually held my own, insisting, for example, that attending a party in a town an hour's drive away was out of the question, but at times I capitulated merely on account of her physical presence— the woman emerging from the child, the unfeminine woman I had not expected; the commanding, demanding woman who made everyone else, including her mother and her older brother, seem so much weaker.

On one October afternoon, I had come home from work early, the commute from the city to Stayner easier than normal, so I decided to pick Charlotte and Sasha up from school to save them the bus ride.

"Can I drive?" Charlotte asked me, coming around to my side of the car as I pulled up to the curb where they had been waiting for the bus. Seventeen, she had recently got her beginner's licence.

"Not today, get in the other side," I said, in a cheerful enough tone.

"Dad . . ." she whined and stood her ground. "Why not?"

"Because I said so," I snapped, sounding the gong on my parenting skills. "You haven't done much on the highway; there's too much traffic today," I added, trying harder.

"I've done highway," she said, with a smirk that told me she'd driven on it with others. "All my friends in Toronto have been driving for a year. They do the Don Valley, the 401, all of it. We're complete hicks up here, Dad." She continued to stand at my door, waiting for me to back down.

"Nope," I said, and started to roll up the window. Defeated, Charlotte turned on her heels in a huff and got in the back seat, letting Sasha, for once, ride shotgun.

"I'm moving back to Toronto," Charlotte said, as she pulled the back door shut.

Sasha was giddy with her day's activities: drama class, the soccer team, and the upcoming auditions for the musical. She talked without breathing for the next ten minutes, as though this exceptional placement up front gave her a unique chance to get it all out, and as if, since the episode with the ecstasy, she was still trying to make up for disappointing us.

"Dad!" Charlotte called out from the back seat, just as I was preparing to change lanes to turn off the highway.

"What?" I asked, slowing down and looking in my rear-view mirror, worried that something was wrong.

"Since when do you go to Fallucci's?"

A spike ran up my chest.

"What are you talking about?" I could see Charlotte in the mirror looking down at something in her hands. My throat went tight. She looked up, caught my eye in the mirror and sat forward.

"Matches?" she asked, all Valley-girl squawky.

"What?" I said stupidly, looking back at the road, changing a lane and signalling to turn right.

"Fancy place, Fallucci's. Rick's parents go to Toronto once a month especially. His uncle owns it."

I pulled onto the two-lane highway that would take us to our sideroad. I felt sick.

"You been there?" she said in a way that wasn't a question. A subtle debating team tactic.

"No."

"Where did these matches come from then?"

"I don't know."

"You don't know." That tone of voice again. I looked into the rear-view mirror and caught her glare.

"Maybe they're Mom's," Sasha said, her thin legs squirming beneath the skirt she hated wearing.

"I don't know," I said and sped the car up a little, then rolled down my window, hoping the wind would shush my elder daughter.

"Mom has never been there. I told her about Rick's parents going. She said she wanted to go too."

— 88 —

"Maybe Fred . . ." I said, like a pitiable fool. Fred had rarely been in our car since he'd got his licence and saved up for his own run-down Toyota.

"Mmmmph," Charlotte grunted, and for a moment I hoped she would let the matter drop. "Why would Fred leave them in your back seat?"

"I don't know, Charlotte. Just stop this inane conversation," I said, exploding now with the aggression of guilt. "You've barely said hello to me, and certainly haven't thanked me for the fact that you don't have to sit on a hot bus that takes three times as long to get home," I was ranting. "And not a word about your day. What's gotten into you?" I didn't look in the rear-view as I turned right onto our concession road, but I knew that Charlotte's face was full of loathing.

I spent the rest of the day swallowing discomfort, wondering if Christine had dropped the matches in the back seat on purpose. I was on the verge of confessing everything to Anna that night, wanting to waylay Charlotte raising the topic, but she never said another word about it.

Christine stayed awake each night after I left, she told me. Over and over again, she blamed me for the insomnia she said was aging her. And for her childlessness. After the hunger, the fumbling, the mad excavation to the centre of her, I would pull out and come somewhere on her body, in my hand or on the sheets. And each night after I left, she'd stay awake alone, aging with an empty womb.

I was playing a perilous game with myself. With her.

"I love my family," I would say, toying with them, too.

"Then what are you doing here wasting my time?" she finally asked one night.

"Well, I love you too," I said, believing in the cliché of the man I had become.

"Go home," she said, and thus it began: the slow attrition of pride and lust. She threatened never to see me again, telling me that at thirty-eight she was now too old to be playing this game. When I called the next day, wracked that she might now hate me, she had softened, and our routine of dinner, sex and songs began again, and at first seemed as spontaneous and erotic as in the beginning. But over the next few months I turned into an observer of myself, wondering how I had come to this, how I could have these conversations, or listen to this pathetic singing. I watched when we fucked, too, wanting someone else to see me, wanting to perform this for an audience, feeling my leg muscles swell, my arms bulge with effort that I wanted documented. I'd do my little show for myself, and then I'd pull out at the very last second.

Charlotte is helping Anna make more piles. They are in our bedroom, and I have come to stand in the doorway to watch. Charlotte has delicately trimmed Anna's hair to an ear-length bob, which will facilitate the clipping and shaving that will take place before they carve open her skull. This small act of vanity in the face of the operation's brutality is something I believe is only possible among women: my daughter is anointing her mother's body in preparation for its mutilation.

"Look at this!" Charlotte yelps, coming across a plaid skirt in Anna's closet. She hauls the skirt out and holds it up to her waist, drawing attention to its extravagant length and bulk. "Good grief, Mom, how could you?"

Anna smiles and puts down the other clothes she has been sorting. She crosses the room to Charlotte. "Ah, I love this skirt; it's so old," she says, fondling the woollen pleats, and both Charlotte and I are drawn in by her perfect syntax.

"You do?" Charlotte says through laughter.

"I do."

"But Mom, it's hideous. It has to go. I'll buy you a new one, after. Shorter, funkier. You'd look great in Vivienne Westwood."

"No, this one," Anna says, without taking her eyes or hands off the plaid, "this one he made in the poppies." Charlotte and I don't even bother to look at one another.

"The tail in the squares makes the bones dance . . . it was that time when all the bones danced." She pulls the skirt tightly against herself and I wonder if this statement is indeed true and not a confabulation.

I have noticed that, but for brief snatches of clarity, Anna's language has changed in the last few days. It feels not so much like a sluicing of random words, but rather a controlled, matter-of-fact absurdity. I imagine that it's not just memories she has confabulated; she is constructing the future now. The moment when all the bones will dance.

"They waste stuff," she says in three controlled words, waving her hand at Charlotte, who smiles in sheepish acknowledgement. "They have loads," Anna continues. Another three. "You've spoiled them," she says as she turns to me.

"I've spoiled them?" I say. "I am the only one who ever gave them a curfew, made them do homework." I smile at Anna and watch the smile rise on her own face. "It was always, 'Wait until Dad gets home.' You gave them money every time they held out their hands!"

"That's true, Mom," Charlotte contributes.

"Don't mind me," I say, laughing, enjoying the three of us this way. "I just went to work, faithfully, every day, to give you all these little extravagances," and I hear my voice catch with regret and hope to God that neither of them has noticed, "and about that, anyway . . ." I am shocking myself, hearing these words come out of my mouth, "about all that . . . work . . . it's something I've been meaning to say, to tell you . . ." and I can sense Charlotte's eyes on me, her brow furrowed in confusion, like mine, "around that time, you know the work was very trying . . . and it's . . ." What am I doing? "It's strange, but I think I must have felt . . ."

I look up at Charlotte, whose lips are pursed so fully in disapproval that they look clownish. We hold each other's gaze for so long I feel my eyes start to get watery.

"Dad, Mom and I aren't finished all this sorting," Charlotte says and gives me a look that says "Over my dead body will you speak now." Yes, Charlotte has known all along, I think. What is this facility with truth that women have?

"Michael Williamson," Anna says as she comes up beside me. "Don't worry, the tear mountains make yellow stripes of us, frozen like the ones in Kyrgyzstan that time the dog bit you."

And I laugh.

Instead of weeping, I laugh so hard that tears come anyway. I take a breath. "I think you're right; we spoiled them," I say. "But at least they've had to find a way to hang on to the lifestyles they grew accustomed to. They're rich! They can look after us." Charlotte looks at the two of us and then walks out of the room. Anna smiles and takes my hand and leads me to the edge of the bed, where we sit.

"If anything—" she starts, but I squeeze her hand so tightly that she stops.

"I think you're supposed to eat a lot of liver when you come out. And carrots. I'm stocking up. Thought I'd make soup too."

From my research and from talking to Gottlieb and others I know every stage and intricate detail of the operation Anna will undergo, from the amount of anaesthetic she will need to the instruments they will use to cut into her. I know far more than I am comfortable with, so instead I focus on liver and carrots.

"Fixing market waves in black leather . . ."

"Lentils, and corn on the cob."

"My driver's licence," she says, returning to her three-fingered accompaniment. She is reminding me that we have to surrender her licence at the hospital. "You'll have to do all the vacuuming—" and I know she means "driving." Or does she? I have grown to enjoy the uncertainty. I am fond of this aneurysm now. Her hands, I notice, are more wrinkled than I remember, and this arouses me.

"I want to show you something," I say, and I get up from the bed and go the drawer of my bureau, where I have hidden little snippets of writing, all the small things I want to tell her, which I promise myself that I will gather and put together into one letter. I catch sight of the words on the top sheet. "I always appreciated when you threw yourself into our life, giving the children things you never had . . ."

These are clumsy, vague imitations of what needs to be said.

When the squalls and frost and minus 20 of January days threw you into your Mediterranean body, you plucked light from a vault and decided to take up cross-country skiing with eight-year-old Fred, who slipped and slid to keep up with you, as you said, "faster, faster, come, we'll stay warm."

I wonder if this is the right way. Perhaps there's a way to be more precise. I retrieve the illustration I began working on last week and finished yesterday. I take it out and close the drawer.

"Here," I say, giving it to her as I sit back down. "Like the old days," I add, and watch as she takes the sheet and examines it.

The light in her face tells me she has understood. I am grateful.

"Slip part of the window under a fountain and off comes the frame," she mutters.

I nod. She's right. Whatever she means, she's right. I can feel her. Everything is perfectly clear. Something new for us when the frame comes off. The past takes too much language. This is how we must proceed.

EIGHT

The lawn mower has stalled. Should I go to the rescue?
I watch through the window of my office as Sasha dis-
mounts the John Deere tractor mower, opens the hood
and peers at the engine, adjusting wires and checking
valves. Her movements are winged and certain. When
I look at her I cannot for the life of me understand why
she has been without a boyfriend for so many years,
or why she isn't married. Charlotte, I know, can be
hard: beautiful, but anodized. Sasha, her face asymmet-
rical, her eyes small yet penetrating, her heart tender,
should be a young man's boon. I think again that it
could be something I've done or not done that keeps

her single—something that has caused this cultivated loneliness which sends her into her own body, so aware yet unknowable. She starts the motor and hops back on the small tractor.

I turn back to my work. I must manage this small feat before the operation. I have something to tell Anna, but I don't yet know how, or even exactly know what it is. If I can get this right, if I stay at this desk and work through the day, and, if necessary, all night, I will glimpse it.

What more than a sex and a pulse—a slow, deep pulse—make a woman? Yes, this is the difficulty. How to represent Anna. Not the me of Anna or the children of Anna. But Anna's essence. Who is she?

"There are magpies in the corn again." She is standing in the doorway.

"Crows," I say, as I turn toward her. I cover the sketch with my hand, stretching out my fingers to slide some opened bills over my handiwork.

"Crows," she repeats. "They shred all the wind in the fountain."

I want to talk to Anna, like this, forever.

"Three greens gobbled in the field, cluttered white clouds two in the sky; the shadows are fences," she says.

Yes, this is true.

I crumple up the sketch, shove it aside, and reach for a clean sheet of paper.

I take my marker and do a quick sketch as she watches over my shoulder.

She takes the sheet of paper and examines it. She smiles. "Mmm," she says, and here we are, for the first time in months, perhaps years, in the same moment, the same way. I see what has been wrong with my previous drawings: my concentration on meaning through a linear process. What Anna and I have in common now is more like a grunt. I need to think more like a cave painter.

I hold her hand as I get up and walk with her outside. The July corn is like a teenager, gawky and nearly as tall as it ever should be, but with the dangerous possibility that it will keep growing. The ears are bulging like oblong testes, and silking has begun: that spurt of thin tassels at the crown of the husk, like the crystallized dregs from a boy's dream. We stand looking out onto the field and I think of the old couple in the painting *American Gothic*— the man grasping his pitchfork, that look of disaffection on their faces from the toil of everything between and around them, everything that makes their lives so fucking hard. I have my marker in my back pocket, and I am standing next to a woman who is stripped of the language that once defined her. We are all that is left of our past and the future.

"I don't want you to have the operation."

But I don't turn to her as I say this. I stare at the corn spewing in its ecstasy, and I wonder if she and I should run through it.

"What?" She turns and faces me.

"There is, there's a chance these symptoms will disappear on their own," I say. It's all lies, all diversion, all desperate keening.

"Michael," she says, and touches the outside of my arm with her hand. "Michael—"

"Martinique!" I blurt out to stop her. "We could go to Martinique. I know it's summer, but we could stay till winter, we—"

"Don't!" she shouts, and I listen for an echo but there is none; the corn has absorbed it. "Owls. The wife ate the owls by mistake, but the trees made holes in her."

"Anna, please, we could take a trip, really. Florida, to see your brother—" and I know this is a dead end, as there's no pretending that seeing Joe would be relaxing for her. She hasn't even told him about the operation. She has no reason to visit the States, and so before she floods on about oranges and grapefruit and Mickey Mouse, I quickly take her arm and draw her into a dance. I find myself singing Tom Jones, "But for me they shine within your eyes . . . As the trees reach for the sky above . . . So my arms reach out to you for love . . . With your hand, resting in mine . . ." I sway with her until she starts to snigger.

And then she stops and pushes me away. "Michael." Her tone is harsh.

"What?" I am a hurt, silly little boy. For some reason I think of Mustafa in Luxor, and an Egyptian ideogram comes to mind: a man on one bended knee, a hand to his mouth as though he's eating, a curve that looks like a fragment of Horus's eye before him, and below that, near his knees, an oblong shape like a cushion on a pedestal. It is the ideogram for love, wish, want, desire. But this sign cannot possibly represent all of those disparate emotions. What is supposed to be obvious is not obvious at all. I want suddenly to get back to my desk to work out a new idea.

"Fixing up the second barn is something I've been planning to do. Put windows in the barn loft, make it a place for the grandchildren," she says, and I think she's speaking remarkably clearly, and that I am right: she doesn't need the operation. "Gold eyes in the glimmers," she continues. It's a delicate mistake. She is better, I tell myself.

"We will do all that, yes, and maybe China . . . we could go to China, you know; we could even sky dive, scuba dive, dive and dive and dive . . ." and I am delirious.

She punches me in the arm.

When I rub it she takes another swing and hits my ribs, then lands another over my kidneys.

"What?" I ask in pain. Her two fists come at me now. Girl punches at my chest, and then on my forearms when I raise them in self-defence. She hates me now, I'm convinced, and it's finally now, this moment, when I've been so stupid, that she will tell me she knows, that she knew all along, and could in fact recite what Christine said to me on that last night, nearly three years into our relationship, when she saw me for the despicable coward I really was. Anna is about to tell me what Christine said then; she is about to say, "you deserve nothing that you have."

I let Anna hit me until she exhausts herself and flops into my arms.

She doesn't cry. I don't cry. I smell her hair.

When I came home from Fallucci's that first time and smelled of cigarettes, not mine—their rusty perfume on my shirt—you told me that there were ways of talking to one another that would not sting. I didn't want to understand what you meant, and believed you had found me out. Worse, I wanted you to know. Wanted to punish you with the knowledge of how I'd lifted her leg, placed it on my shoulder to angle in, just so. Wanted you to know how lost I had become.

Anna wipes her nose into my shirt. "You want me to die," she says gently, clearly, raising her face now, which is tear-stained and snotty.

Dear God. I hold onto her and feel the slippery wetness on my shirt.

"Anna, please, I'm frightened." And I take her face in my hands and see that there's no fear there. Her eyes say that she wants me to do better than that.

"Let's go to the market," I say, thinking I'd like to cook something special for her tonight. As we walk towards the car, I feel how death has made my every action suspect. Either I have a duty to tell her everything or no right at all to taint her memory with my version of reality. I have no idea which of these choices is the right one.

Later, Anna's shallow breathing tells me that she is only pretending to sleep in order to be left alone. And I am at work again. The corn feels close, like hair curling at my neck. A hot breeze blows through the rows tonight and the moon is growing back its broken face. The horses in the field are running, and their canter beats a rhythm in my head. When I close my eyes, filaments of light behind the lids dance like the aurora borealis. I'm desperate to get it right, but it isn't yet.

The question of duty brings me to this point: where what I am meets what I say I am. And here be dragons, as the map-makers used to write. I can tell Anna what she doesn't know, or tell her more of what she does. Does she know I was a man who split his life in two for fear of ending up with nothing? Does she understand how such cowardliness can last so long?

NINE

"Dad, there's toast—take some toast," Charlotte says as I nibble on the scrambled eggs she has prepared.

"Good eggs," Fred says, his lips making that wet-smacking sound that convinces me he cannot be my son. I push away my plate. My children are vulgar, devouring food in front of their mother when they know she has been on "nil by mouth" since midnight. Sasha has at least taken hers outside to eat on the porch.

I touch my pocket and feel the crumpled sheet there. It's shit, this drawing. It will not do. The head is all wrong, the feet out of proportion. If these selfish children would just get out of our way, I could find the time to get it right. And maybe even convince Anna that the whole trip to

Toronto isn't necessary. If I'm to lose her, I want it to be here, on my turf, in our own house, with enough time for both of us to speak, or not to speak, or—

"I've just heard from Rosie, she'll be on shift by the time we get there," Fred says.

Fred, I must admit, has been stellar about dealing with the hospital. He's made special arrangements for a particular attendant at St. Michael's, a nurse named Rosie, who will give Anna that extra bit of care.

Sasha comes back inside with her plate as Charlotte scrapes some charring off a piece of toast. I hear Anna upstairs in the washroom, preparing to come down.

"Finish up and clear the table," I say generally to these overgrown bodies. I feel Charlotte's eyes on me. I look up at Sasha, who has traced the agitated motion inside me to the trembling in my cheek.

Dear Anna, when we returned from Egypt the shadows on the rim of my eyelids made shapes like the leaves of all the varieties of lettuce on earth. The leaves were veined with all the lies of my life. I watched them, and followed.

"Dad, Uncle David called; he wants you to call him after the operation," Sasha says, picking up my plate from the table. Charlotte rises with her own plate and joins her sister at the sink. "He sounded like he meant it," Sasha adds, and looks at me with daughter-pity for her old dad who doesn't know how to maintain a relationship with his only brother. They both lean on the counter, facing me.

"Suzanne called me yesterday," Charlotte says, and coils a ringlet from Sasha's hair gently around her finger so gently that I wonder if she feels like I do, like anything we touch right now will snap. "She said David wanted to come, but I told her that wasn't necessary." When she drops the ringlet she runs the back of her fingers along Sasha's neck the way a lover might, and I feel ignorant of my own flesh and blood.

"Come on, hurry up," I say, crotchety. Since when does Charlotte have the right to stop putting Aunt and Uncle in front of Suzanne and David?

"Dad, relax," Charlotte says, and she stops caressing Sasha's neck and throws her own straight mane over her shoulder in a gesture so like her mother's that I feel dizzy. "We've got two hours."

"That's not that much time, with traffic down the 400..."

"Chill, Dad," Fred says, and I know he never uses that word in his daily life but is performing for his sisters.

"Since when are you so easygoing about time?" I ask, tasting the grit in my own voice. I imagine the hatchet, its glistening blade sharp as a guillotine, which I would take now to some living thing. Fred rolls his eyes at me and picks up his plate as he rises and takes it to the sink.

"What?" I ask.

Fred doesn't answer me, but I see how he shakes his head at Charlotte as he clears space for his dishes.

"Charlotte," I start, but I have no idea what it is I need to say. I grasp at an old idea. "What is the latest on the car? Have you made a decision?" These are the kinds of things I used to attend to for them, the things they count on me for—the car, tax returns, mortgages. For them I have no inner life. Charlotte needs a new car to replace her old Lexus, a gas guzzler, and she should know better, but it's up to me: "A hybrid is the best bet with the price of oil—" and I stop myself because I haven't been following the price of oil, but I know it's outrageous, and the idea of a car, of getting one, of putting my wife in one to take her to this operation, makes me feel so nauseated that I have to hold my head up with my hands.

"Dad," Charlotte is at my side in a flash. "Dad, are you okay?" I stare at her. "You were swaying."

"Don't you go on us now," says Fred in a cheery, I'll-have-to-do-everything-then voice.

"Who the fuck said anyone was going?" I say.

There is a putrid smell coming up from between my legs. I am revolting.

"Who said anyone was going anywhere?" I repeat, and Charlotte must smell it too because she backs away from me. There's a rodent silence now, a skittering away to stillness.

"What?" I ask, looking up at each of them. First Fred, with his air of casual control that says he will never be the fool of a man I have become. I wonder who he is fucking these days to make him feel so smug. For him I gave up mornings alone with my wife, where I was safe, when the crow of day meant that all I had to do was roll over and plant myself inside her. For him I put on a tie. Then Charlotte, second born and yet the first to make me want to keep secrets: petty secrets like leaving half an hour early for work, just to be away from home half an hour longer, or pretending to read the paper so that no one would talk to me.

But when I look at Sasha . . . the hatred is rightfully aimed at my own breast.

I stand.

"Map the tunes in the hairbrush," Anna says over my left shoulder, startling me as I dry my hands on a dish-towel. The cloth is filthy; it hasn't been replaced for weeks. I turn to face her and see that she is indeed holding a hairbrush, and I see, with this new way of knowing, that Anna is perfectly fine, and right to want to examine the wave capacity of important objects as she prepares her head for the assault that is about to take place.

"Mom," says Fred, walking towards his mother, his voice a pinwheel of fear. I see him as he was: the little boy who made airplanes out of matchbox covers and napkins at restaurants to which he'd been dragged because his father had insisted upon civilized evenings out as a break from the tedium of domesticity. But Fred knew then what I am only beginning to comprehend. He knew that the best moments are silent, and unmeasured but for the task at hand.

Charlotte comes up behind me and runs water in the sink as she starts the dishes, so I don't hear what Fred says next, but a moment later Anna laughs. She reaches out to her son, who is standing between us and blocking my view. Her hand rises up to touch his face; her fingers push back the hair at his temples and caress the side of his head. I struggle to remember the last time Anna touched my face.

The kitchen smells cheesy; there is filth in the corners.

"Take your time, Mom," Fred says as he grabs her hand and holds it. "You're not scheduled until noon. I'll call them if you want . . ." and his voice trails off in that pinwheel flutter, and I am surprised that reliable, punctual, rule-abiding Fred would put his reputation at stake for his mother's comfort.

But surprise feels normal now.

How did I get here?

"Sweetheart." I walk to Anna, not knowing what else to do. She must be starving, parched. There's nothing to offer but my presence beside her. "Let's go upstairs. I'll get your bag and you can lie down for a few minutes if you need to."

"Not lie down," Anna says. She looks at me, flustered, and then looks around as though she's searching for something I haven't brought with me. "I need those nozzles, the ones they put on the juniper bush." She points to my drawing pad on the table, and I realize that she expects us to talk in that new way. My heart sinks; I have nothing to show her. "Magnum feebleness popping—"

"Right," I say, cutting her off, taking her arm and leading her upstairs. I leave Fred and the girls staring at one another in the kitchen.

"Told you, it embarrasses him," Charlotte says to her siblings.

The skin on my face prickles.

TEN

I remember a day in Cairo.

Anna was out in the shops, searching for fine cotton and linen. I had made an excuse of the heat, saying she would get more out of the shopping if I wasn't there to complain. I told her I would finish the book she had bought me, Durrell's *Alexandria Quartet*, in the quiet cool of our room and then meet her for lunch. But I had been irritated with the book from the moment I had begun it on the airplane, and had only skimmed it during those Luxor afternoons by the pool. I couldn't face it again, so went down to the hotel front desk, where I chatted with the concierge about a restaurant for lunch. He told me about a café in old Cairo where Naguib Mahfouz, Egypt's

Nobel Prize-winning author, used to write. I remember feeling disloyal to Anna as I stood listening to the man describe the great writer's Cairo Trilogy and the profound influence the novels had on him, because, after all, books were her territory. I asked him where I could buy a copy, and he directed me to the hotel gift shop. I tucked the copy of *Palace Walk* under my shirt as I left the shop, as though I had something to hide—not from the authorities who had banned it in many Arab countries, but from Anna. I walked up the four flights of stairs to the rooftop terrace, where I sat alone in the scorching sun, prepared to be entranced by the book.

It was 11:55; I know because I had just checked my watch to see how much time I had before our planned lunch at one. I would enjoy this hour alone. As I began to read—"She woke at midnight. She always woke up then without having to rely on an alarm clock,"—there came in successive waves from all directions in the streets below, a sound whose horn-like crescendo made me think of a battle cry. It was the clamouring voices of men, the marauding bellows of invaders riding on horseback over the desert, surrounding the city, and descending upon Cairo in a moaning tide of agony and elation to take its citadel and rejoice in its women.

I realized that the sound was in fact the rising call to prayer from all the mosques in the city, the chorus of voices amplified up on the terrace, their elation swelling inside me, drawing me forward. As I looked at the clear blue sky, containing only a single cloud, and as the call got steadily louder, I imagined the mosques filling, the muezzin's call herding the sleepy market traders and toiling farmers, rescuing its lonesome slum dwellers. At that moment, the lone cloud passed before the sun. I sat up straight in my lounge chair and took the occlusion as an ominous sign, and suddenly felt smug in my skepticism among these believers.

Three minutes later the sound was gone. I put down *Palace Walk* with a hunger in me that felt like a weapon. I wanted to find something that would take me out of myself, out of my marriage, out of this thing that was sharp and hot and grinding inside me. I walked out into Cairo's streets.

Now, I make my way through the stale, pale hospital corridor in search of her again, feeling blunt, harmless. I find her room, pause, then enter.

She is bald.

I put my briefcase down on the floor beside the door and go to her. My wife is sitting up in the bed. Her hospital gown is the tint of a faded asparagus fern, and she is now a shaven captive of Ontario's sandy soil, not the dark banana-leaf princess I first met.

"It's fine," I say, stupidly, as I lean down and kiss her cheek. She hasn't asked me, hasn't even indicated that the baldness is an issue for her. She pats my hand. There is a small bubble of skin at the nape of her neck that I have never seen before and it reminds me of a wet, shivering animal.

Rosie, the Filipino nurse that Fred arranged for, comes in to take Anna's blood pressure. She has been carefully monitoring every one of Anna's vital signs and has given her the final Hunt and Hess assessment. This scale is the neurological indicator of the severity of the condition based on the patient's symptoms. It allows the doctors to prepare for the operation; to know how they will deal with the aneurysm and the pressure on the brain as a result of swelling. Anna is at Grade 2-, which is a good sign. She has not suffered paralysis, although she seems to have a stiff neck. She is alert, aware of her surroundings, and her speech is not any worse than it has been in the last week.

"Feed the dogs," she says to me and pats my hand again. I stare at her. We haven't had a dog since our family retriever, Miko, was run over on Highway 12 almost fifteen years ago.

"I will." I return to my briefcase, which has fallen over. I set it right and consider getting out the pad, a fresh piece of paper, as I'm not ready yet to show her the one I've been working on. A creeping foolishness wakes me up. Who do I think I am kidding? What did I think I would accomplish with this little gesture? My absolution? This is possibly the most cowardly act of all. I should have completed that letter, written down the exact words, and been a man while I awaited the consequences. At the very least I should have strung together those snippets of words in the drawer and tagged on the appropriate conclusion: forgive me.

"Stop it," a voice says behind me, and it's Charlotte

speaking to Sasha, who is laughing as they come into the room from their small excursion to a Queen Street café for the Blue Mountain coffee that Sasha says is the best in town. I click the clasps of the briefcase back in place and leave it propped up against the wall. I join them by the bed. Fred has returned to his hospital to check in on an elderly patient he was assigned yesterday, and somehow I'm relieved that all I have to deal with in this room are these three women.

"Shit!" Charlotte says as she takes in Anna's bald head.

"Your head's a perfect shape, Mom," says Sasha.

"Braised harps strung in trees—"

"Mom," Sasha interrupts her mother gently, "I bought you some nail polish. Charlotte and I are going to do your nails. We have time. I really never have seen such a perfect shape. I wonder if mine would look like that if I shaved it."

"Do you remember, Mom, we did this when I had my tonsils out," Charlotte says, taking on her sister's gentleness as she pulls out the polish and some cotton balls.

For six months after it ended, I ached for her—for her, and for the roaring sound that had rushed through me. But slowly I got the knack of this deadpan muttering.

I wonder if Fred has really had to return to work or if he's off fucking the woman he's obviously been seeing. And what if I were to tell everything to Anna now, before she leaves this room for the surgery? Tell her how I never knew that defiance and betrayal would feel so fucking great?

I will the girls to leave. I pretend to be packing up myself by going to my briefcase and opening it.

"Charlotte has been flirting with the male nurse," Sasha says to Anna in a playful voice.

"I have not!"

"You think because he does something un-macho that he'll be great in bed—I know you."

"Sash!"

"That's what you thought about Robert."

"Robert was good in bed!"

They laugh. I take paper out of the briefcase, then the drawing I did last night. I hesitate, then snap shut the briefcase with my free hand.

"In the desert there was one street light near our hut at the oasis. The Bedouin who danced with me had three wives."

I turn and look up at Anna's face, her head, round and then tapered towards her neck like a light bulb. I know that what she has just said is not confabulation. This really happened. I was there.

"She asked him if he minded night shifts," Sasha says.

"That's not flirting," Charlotte defends.

"Ha!"

"His hips—they tossed themselves at me like a woman's," Anna says, and the girls don't exactly ignore her but neither do they take what she's saying seriously. Only I know that Anna is right. The man moved like a belly dancer.

Before everything changed.

Cairo had been a layover between the Upper Nile—Mustafa and the Valley of the Kings—and the next leg of our holiday in the desert. We were picked up at our hotel by a driver and another man I thought was to be our translator, but upon attempting to communicate with them it was clear that neither could speak English. The extra passenger, I realized, was the driver's friend along for the ride. He took advantage of the minivan's sound system to play tapes of Arabic music at high volume for the entire five-hour trip. As we drove past various formations of desert sand and rock, fantastical mushrooms, giant drums, and hundreds of dunes that resembled the backs of house-sized beetles skittering along the brown sand, I felt drugged, kidnapped, by the men and the chant-like singing blaring from the speakers.

We arrived in one of the towns of the Bahariya Oasis in the western desert of Egypt. I stumbled out of the van, fatigued and disoriented, and we were led to the home of a Bedouin family whose eldest son, Helal, was known, the

Cairo concierge had told us, for eventful tours into the White and Western Deserts, and whom we would meet at dinner that evening.

"This is wonderful," Anna said. She pressed her body close to mine as we headed into the modest clay house. "This is what you wanted, and I'm glad you talked me into it." There was only the slightest inflection to convey that she wanted my assurance. She was trying hard. I took a deep breath to help me handle the feel of her against my skin. I was unbearably hot, but it was not the heat of the desert; I was fiery with something under my breath, inside my lungs.

At the house, we met several Bedouin men, introduced to us by their roles: cook, camel tamer, builder, gardener. The last, Hamada—a short, boyish man with a serious face and small eyes—was to be our guide. We were invited to sit on the floor, where he served us a lunch of goat's cheese, cucumber and tuna. Canned tuna in the desert? Though I didn't say anything to Anna, the fact of this was dismaying to me beyond all reason. I watched Anna expertly wrap the flat wood-oven-baked bread around hunks of white cheese and fish, an expertise I was thinking must have been granted to Middle-Eastern people at birth. Hamada nodded at her, produced his first smile since our introduction, and I was irked. But when she faltered, dropped some of the cheese before it reached her mouth, reacting with an "oops" and a smile, I saw how I was wrong, how I'd spent years exoticizing her and how she was just like me. Still, the air in my lungs seared my insides.

After lunch, Hamada took us in a four-by-four on a tour of the oasis, the surrounding desert, and the sudden, astonishing gardens carved out of the land, where men irrigated crops with water flowing into gutters around vegetable patches and small orchards. At the base of a palm tree Hamada leapt up several times before he succeeded in grabbing hold of a low branch, which he shook with vigour until dark, oblong pods fell to his feet. He bent down and collected the pods in his tunic, then approached Anna, who took one from him. He moved towards me, but I put up my hand to refuse.

"Dates," Anna said, as she sucked on one, her mouth puckered as though over a nipple. I hesitated, took one, and tasted its burly sweetness. As they walked ahead of me toward the Jeep I heard laughter from Anna, and was curious as to what the so far dispassionate Hamada might have said to provoke it. I noticed that Anna and Hamada were a similar height. Had Anna not been raised in Canada would she have been married off to a more suitable-sized, duskier-skinned man like Hamada? I drew a gasping breath, tossed the rest of the pulpy date on the ground and followed them. I was eager to get to the camp. There, I felt, I'd be able to breathe, to relax into the landscape and disappear into myself without any of the social niceties that this part of the tour required.

At the end of the day, after sitting us on a blanket at the edge of the oasis and feeding us corn that had been roasted over an open fire and a red tea made from sorrel leaves, Hamada drove us toward the outer perimeter of the Black

Desert to our camp. We were greeted by the expedition's leader, Helal, who had been born in the desert, was committed to its preservation, and was delighted to share its beauty with the right kind of people. I watched as Anna greeted him; how certain he seemed, merely by the look of her, that she was the right kind of people.

The camp was run entirely by men between, I guessed, twenty and thirty years of age; slim, statuesque men dressed in knee-length light-blue cotton shirts with matching trousers, barefoot or sandaled, with turbans on their heads; beautiful men who clapped to the music of horns and tarabuka drums even if it came from a tape in a car. I saw no women.

That night we ate an elaborate dinner with the men, seated on mats at a low table in a one-roomed, spacious sandstone building, where we were served bowls of tomato, eggplant, lentils, rice, and one of "meat," as it was described to Anna when she asked. Two German couples were the only other tourists there and after dinner we all joined in a circle with Helal, Hamada and the others.

The cold desert night had descended and I desperately wanted to be under the camel blanket I noticed had been laid across the bed in our small hut in the dunes. I squirmed closer to the coal fire in the centre of the room and felt Anna follow me, snuggling close, as though attached by an invisible rope. To distract myself I tried to engage the Germans, but their poor facility with English and my non-existent German soon led to polite nodding and turning again to the music the men began to play.

Helal played a lute-like guitar, Hamada a tambourine-like drum. Helal sang a line, the other men answered in a Bedouin call and response that sounded personal and yet warlike. The music swirled around us as I leaned in closer and closer to the fire.

Suddenly, but without missing a beat, Hamada passed his drum to the tribesman on the right and stood, taking up a scarf from the sandy floor, which he tied around his hips.

And how he danced.

I call it dancing now, but when he began I thought it must be a mating ritual. His hips pulsed, slowly, erotically, from side to side, back and forth, and he held his arms up above his head and closed his eyes as though he were making love to a spirit that stood before him. And I was sure that ghost had Anna's shape.

She sat straight, attentive, with a broad smile on her face that made her eyes sink deeper behind the folds of the Asian dusks and dawns that had created her. A young man stood up, this one much younger than Hamada, only a boy really, and he danced in front of Hamada with a similar rolling, lolling, hip-diving movement. The performance made me even more uncomfortable.

"They were so beautiful," Anna said to me later, as I shivered in the flannel pyjamas I'd wisely brought for these desert nights. She wrapped her leg around me, trying to make both of us warm.

"Well, I guess so, but a little weird," I said, rigid in my spot on the bed.

She looked up towards me: "Weird?"

"You didn't think so?"

I sensed her frown. Her leg slid off mine. I'd disappointed her. She had been trying so hard. I knew that deep down she would rather have been home with our children, but here she was, trying, like a pet, to awaken my attention.

"Such confidence in the movement, so masculine," she said.

I swallowed. A dark listlessness descended. I sank into a deep chamber of ennui. And felt it would be impossible to get out of it.

The next day, with Helal off on a separate tour with the Germans, Hamada drove us across the architectural dunes of the Black Desert, then farther along the edge of the Western Desert en route to the White Desert. The road was lined by desert sculpture—hardened sandy mounds sprinkled with black rock. The shapes were like darker cousins to the skittering beetle mounds we'd seen en route, but suddenly, everything was white. I can only liken our final destination to what the bottom of the sea would look like without the water or the life that thrives in it. The White Desert is nature's sculpture garden, filled with crisp, bleached white sandstone figures that resembled a rabbit here, an eagle there, a mushroom over there. Odd sprouted mushrooms, with crowns formed from what looked like the finest marble, dotted the landscape.

We drove through the desertscape, stopping to marvel at spectacular formations, to pick up desert crystals and to walk on this alien terrain. A scorching, stalagmite planet.

"Look, look!" Anna said as we drove towards another pasture of rock.

"Ah," Hamada said, smiling, pointing to where she was staring, both of them fixed on the same object. We pulled up beside an oblong sandstone figure that seemed to have been hollowed out. Hamada was delighted that Anna had spotted it without prompting. He got out of the Jeep first and walked toward the stone object with reverence. I got out next, happy to stretch my legs. Anna seemed to be stuck in her seat, transfixed. What we were all staring at looked familiar, but I couldn't quite put my finger on what it was.

"A whale," Anna said, as she opened the door and walked past me. I watched and then followed her, going right up to the carved out figure.

"They have measured it. Archaeologists. Equal to actual whale. Real ones," Hamada said. I looked at him incredulously.

"Oh my goodness," Anna intoned.

"Look here," Hamada said as he took us inside the stone husk through its missing head. He rubbed the wall with his hands. I copied him automatically, feeling what he had intended me to feel: the ridges that were surely once the ribcage of the whale. I sat down. How was this possible here in the desert? Eventually, Anna and Hamada walked back to the Jeep, but I continued to sit in the belly of the whale, for some moments longer.

As we travelled into the desert, the afternoon sun rendered the white stone brittle-looking, as though it might chip away with a gust of wind. We drove across dunes dotted with iron ore deposits that had formed into dark crystals, metal flowers popping up through the desert sand. The world was inside out and upside down.

I sat in the back seat of the Jeep; Anna sat in front, asking questions of Hamada as he drove, over the Arabic music that floated from the tape player. After some miles, the Jeep started to sputter and jerk. Hamada stepped hard on the gas, in an attempt to override the problem. Slowing and then hard again. And again, but the Jeep stuttered to a halt.

Hamada walked to the front of the Jeep, opened the hood and examined the engine. He unhooked the hose which led from the engine to the tank, inspecting it before going to the back of the Jeep, where he dug out some rubber piping. Returning to the engine, he leapt onto the edge of the Jeep's frame, inserted the pipe and devised a siphon, which, he explained, would let him extract the water that had been added to stretch the cheap black-market fuel.

"That is normal for Egypt," he said as he brought the stiff pipe to his mouth and held it firmly between his lips. I felt my knee buckle ever so slightly as he sucked. Anna observed him without emotion, taking in the angle of the pipe in his mouth, presumably grateful that Hamada was saving us from a cruel death of scorching, starvation and blindness.

I stepped forward.

"Anything I can do to help?" I knew about cars, having grown up with auto parts strewn about the fields next to our farmhouse near Kleinburg. My father loved getting under the hood of our Ford, always ready to communicate his deep pleasure in the way things connected: plugs and oil and carburetor and ignition.

Hamada said nothing, of course, and how foolish of me to have expected him to, with that thing in his mouth. Anna did not take her eyes off his lips.

"Do you remember, Anna?" I say, and I realize that she and I are alone in the hospital room now. I shove the blank paper and drawing in my hands into my jacket pockets. I have no idea where Charlotte and Sasha have gone. Probably off to torture the male nurse—all of them with this power to give such delightful pain.

Anna looks at me, as though she too has just remembered that I'm in the room.

"The desert night. The fox we heard around the tent," I say.

She stares and seems to be searching her memory. Was I wrong? Had she not been referring to Hamada just now?

"Anna," I say again. She moves her mouth as if to speak, but I see how she stops herself. She shakes her head.

She stares.

I wait.

"Anna, please!" I am beginning to lose control.

I look towards the door, dismayed by my own tone. How fortunate we are that my insurance has paid for this private room, where I can yell at my wife with impunity, minutes before she is to have her head sliced open. For God's sake. My head falls into my hands.

"Everything okay in here?" a thin, delicate nurse says from the doorway. I look up and nod. Anna smiles at her and waves, and the woman retreats with relief.

"Anna, I'm so sorry," I say.

She shakes her head, still refusing to speak, and I think it's for fear that I will shout at her again.

I sit on the bed and begin to cry. Anna raises her hand towards my face, but I intercept it with my own hand. I put my other hand on her shoulder.

"I meant the night in Egypt. Remember how cold it was?"

She nods, but I don't think she does remember. I can feel that cold right now as I stroke Anna's hand. Her eyes close. Perhaps she is falling asleep. I keep stroking.

As the sun sank in the White Desert, the sky turned the colour of a cantaloupe. We drove a few more un-sputtering miles, the Jeep's fuel now cleansed of the destructive water.

We searched for a suitable site to stop for the night, and eventually pulled up in the shelter of a bleached sandstone beetle. Hamada unpacked and began to set up camp. I looked on, helpless, knowing better than to offer assistance, but Anna didn't suffer from the same inhibition. I watched as she took out our food supply and laid out the vegetables on the grand Bedouin rug that would be our dining room that evening. While Hamada tended the fire, slowly turning sticks to even out the flame, waiting for the wood to become ash and charcoal, and then repeating the cycle, Anna began to peel potatoes and then wash them in a basin with water from the plastic jug that Hamada had set down beside her. It was as though they had done this hundreds of time before, together.

"Here," he said, after noticing she was struggling to make the knife work without a cutting board or hard surface. He took the knife from her, held a potato in his other hand, and with a movement that looked like the delicate polishing of a stone, the potato was diced, magically. I watched Anna's face change like an old-fashioned animation cartridge—each minute gesture captured in successive frames: Anna curious, Anna bemused, Anna wary, Anna delighted and Anna radiant.

"Hamada," she said, as though the sound of the syllables gave her pleasure.

He grilled chicken on the fire, as the potatoes boiled over the gas cylinder camp stove. To accompany the meal we had more of the red sorrel tea that I'd quickly grown to love. We ate in silence, I remember. It was my silence,

I realize now, but at the time I was certain that it was theirs. The sky grew dark, but above us the stars were like hundreds of small fires in call and response with our own.

Again at night the desert turned intensely cold. I couldn't step away from the fire without thinking I might die from exposure in a place that just a few hours ago had made me swoon from heat. Hamada made a faint noise—and Anna stirred as though recognizing this as the signal to retire to our tent for the night. Hamada stood and put out the remaining flame in the firepit with his bare foot. I watched Anna turn back in time to catch the last dab of his toe on the log, which he flicked over into the sand, allowing the remaining embers to glow, their faint whisper rising to the stars. I saw her shudder.

I stood and followed her into the small nylon tent, my shoulders twitching with the unbelievable chill of the brittle night.

"God, it's freezing," I said, a statement so obvious that I instantly felt foolish in front of my own wife. I dared to take off my shoes so that I could slide into my sleeping bag, hoping the extra layer would quell my shivering. I looked up and caught Anna's eye; her face gave away nothing.

I heard a noise outside, a kind of skittering that couldn't possibly have been a human. But what then? A snake? A rat? I heard Hamada groan in the distance. His bed of rugs, woven saddlebags and camel blankets was in the open air, under the full canopy of stars, and somehow warm enough for him.

Anna dropped down to her knees. She pawed at the sleeping bag in which I had entombed myself.

"Wasn't that an amazing day," she said. The beam of the flashlight, which was perched on her cosmetics bag, illuminated the corner where the red nylon panels of the side and top met, making our tent look slanted—a lopsided cubist tent.

She pulled my sleeping bag down.

"What are you doing?" I pleaded, grabbing the edge of the bag and holding tight to stop the warmth from escaping. She didn't look up, but I felt her smile. Her silhouette widened, her hand loosened my grip and, leaning her head towards my lap, she pulled the sleeping bag down to my knees.

"Anna," I said, and I thought I heard the skittering outside again, louder this time and possibly human.

"Shhh," she whispered, and touched my face ever-so briefly. She unclasped my belt and slid my fly down. I freed my leg from the sleeping bag and lost track of the skittering sound, then of sound altogether as I swelled at the smell of her hair in the tent, the lopsided angle of her head silhouetted against the nylon wall as she bent over and kissed my cock. And again, gently, one touch of her lips. I throbbed in response. Another kiss. And another.

She took me in her mouth and held on. She swirled her tongue over the small vein at the base of the head, where she knew it would have its greatest effect. And then, suddenly, I pictured Hamada's face, the pipe that led to the gasoline tank, and I softened.

I pushed away the image and focused again on her lips. She took me in deeper than ever, it seemed, and then there was nothing in this world but her mouth.

I came quickly. She swallowed.

I sat up and looked toward her face, feeling the need to apologize, fearing she hated me then.

"Darling," she said, and I felt her face widen again in a smile. "I think a fox has taken the chicken bones."

"What?" I asked.

"You're not cold now," she said, feeling my fingers. She pulled the sleeping bag up around me.

And as my bald wife lies sleeping, in a brief moment of respite from the slow drip that is eroding her faculties, I see her face as first on the list of things that I have never truly trusted. Trust requires a faith, which I have never had, that life will treat me as it should. It requires me to trust death the way I trusted being born.

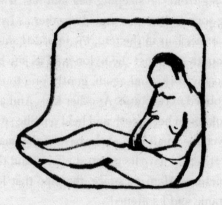

I am not half the man Hamada was: a man with three wives, he was required by the laws of his faith, to care for each equally, provide for each identically, and serve all of them wholly. I gave Christine much less than I have given Anna. I have resisted everything that says that service is freedom and that the small acts of forbearance between two people are . . . are what? They are more than I know.

I don't know her.

She might be going to her death, and I have never known her. Why have I left everything so late?

"Anna," I say, gently, trying to wake her, but not wanting to startle her. "Anna?" I touch the side of her face. Her eyes open and she looks at me as though I've slapped her.

"Melting," she says.

"Can you hear me?"

"Thimbles."

"Sweetheart." I take the hand that she holds out to me. It is shaking.

"Miming—" Again she stops. At least she can stop herself now, I think. If she can control herself, perhaps it's only her tongue that is not working. Her brain, I tell myself, is fine. Is really fine.

"Anna, we're ready for you, dear," says Rosie as she enters, followed by the delicate nurse from earlier.

"Wait!" I say. "Wait." The second time more politely, as I turn to confront her.

Rosie shakes her head at me. "The doctors are ready; we have to go now."

I stand in front of Anna, blocking the nurse's access to the bed.

"We have to go now," Rosie says.

"But the girls aren't here," I say, stalling.

"I'm sorry," Rosie says, and puts her hand on my arm and gently moves me out of the way.

I take last night's drawing from my pocket.

"Break knack picking stick," Anna says. I step forward again and slide the drawing in my hand underneath the edge of her pillow.

"That's right, dear," the nurse says, and for a moment I believe she's telling me I did the right thing, but I feel unravelled.

"Mom," Charlotte says as she enters the room. Anna smiles at her, and then at Sasha, who follows behind.

"Mommy," Sasha says, and we all notice this regression, but not even Charlotte, who is holding onto the shoulder of her mother's hospital gown with a terrified grip, would dare comment now. "You'll be fine. We'll be right here. I can't wait to see you when you wake up," Sasha says, her voice as steady as one of her pirouettes.

Rosie pulls up the brakes on the bed. I lean in and kiss Anna on her lips, and she holds my head to hers. The nurses wait patiently as I release myself from the kiss and smile at my wife.

"Okay, then, we're off," says Rosie, and with a flourish Anna is wheeled out of the room. I catch her face just in time to recognize that she is terrified. I run along behind her towards the operating rooms and stop just as the restricted area doors swing shut. I am suddenly a character in some TV melodrama that I used to mock my children for watching.

ELEVEN

The hospital cafeteria smells like a combination of pro‐cessed cheese and a wet animal. The stench is so appalling that it overwhelms my attempt to come up with a sign for a public eating place.

The people in here look like it smells. For the most part they are pale, stringy and sticky-looking, as though baked at a low temperature for too long.

The napkin I draw on shreds easily; I tear it up. Why didn't I bring my briefcase from Anna's room?

I have been here for nearly forty-five minutes, abandoned once again by my daughters for an errand that involves a scarf for their mother's head, something that "will make her feel pretty," they said, even though their mother might never feel anything again. Fred has chosen not to phone me on my cell, but to call the nurses' station instead, to check in with Rosie. He is keeping his professional cool. The message he left for me said, "Everything going as expected. Will see you in a couple of hours." What does he know about "expected"?

I expect that I will die if my wife does not survive.

By now she has been given the optimal dose of anaesthetic, and her breathing has slowed, her heart rate has dropped. Her brain stays awake; only her mind sleeps. This is the paradox of anaesthesia. Anna is now unconscious but her brain is still able to keep the rest of her body alive as her head is placed in a three-pin skull fixation device. The clamp will hold her head in place while Dr. Gottlieb makes a zigzag incision at the top of the skull.

The clip-clop of my heart becomes a zoom.

I look around me at the stringy, sticky people, and no one else seems to be alarmed. One group, a Punjabi family, stands out. Two young women in silk caftans to their calves, over-wide, patterned trousers, scarves slung around the front of their necks and flowing down their backs, hover around a table where an older woman in more traditional dress, her head covered by her scarf, sits. Next to her, an older man—the grandfather? uncle?—in Sikh turban and with a beard almost as white as his garments, is hunched over, looking miserable. Is it his wife they are visiting? Or his son? Where is the mature woman's husband? She unpacks food from a hamper, unwrapping dish after dish. Wisely, they have brought their own supplies, and I regret my own poor preparation.

When my father died before I met Anna—a sudden heart attack, with one day in the ER, another day in the morgue—I remember wondering if I'd ever have a son to mourn me. I stare at the young women of the family, perhaps the daughters; their placid faces give nothing away.

What will happen to my wife's mind? Over the past month there has been no past between us. All Anna and I have is each moment of now. And in the now I have done nothing wrong. In the now I am exonerated.

"Dad," Charlotte says. Startled, I snap my plastic spoon in two and spill coffee on the table. I see a sliver of blood surface on my thumb. I look up. Charlotte and Sasha are sitting across from me. I wonder how long they have been there.

"Where were you?" Charlotte says, all chippy and choppy, and I wonder if she means just now or all along?

"We were upstairs looking for you," Sasha says. "Have you had anything to eat? Do you want lunch?"

"I'm starving," Charlotte says. "But the food here is complete crap. I may have to settle for a donut. For the first time in about ten years."

When she is gone, I'm alone with Sasha and relieved. But Sasha is scrutinizing my face. "Mom's stronger than she seems sometimes," she says.

"Who would know that better than I do?" I say. "But they're ruining her right now."

"What?"

"Right now," I say, and look at my watch and determine it is around this moment that Dr. Gottlieb will be making a skin incision to expose Anna's skull. The skin and muscles are being lifted off the bone and folded back. A drill will bore holes into the skull that will allow the craniotome, a special saw, an entry to cut through bone. "The aneurysm has shown her off. Maybe that's really her."

Sasha's face betrays the fear of a daughter whose father as well as mother is now potentially lost to her.

"I just mean that maybe interference is unnatural."

Sasha looks at me with horror.

"I mean . . . her mind . . . she's less articulate, but maybe more lucid . . ." I mumble, but I know that I've lost her now. I didn't mean to frighten her. "Aren't you going to eat something? We have a while yet."

"I'm fine," she says.

"This place is gross," Charlotte says as she comes back to our table. "Let's go out for a bite. We have a couple more hours before we'll hear anything."

"No, no. I'm staying here," I say, adamantly.

"Me too," says Sasha.

"But, guys, we—"

"Right about now your mother has a jigsaw in her skull carving out the bone like it's a pop-out window!" My voice is much louder and harsher than I had intended.

"Come on, Sash," Charlotte says, as she grabs her sister by the sleeve, pulling her up from the table. They walk out of the cafeteria with Charlotte's arm draped protectively over Sasha's shoulder.

I leave the cafeteria, dropping crumpled sheets of paper into the garbage can on the way out. I avoid the elevator and instead take the stairs to the third floor. A young man in his twenties, with brown hair and strong arms, shoots up ahead of me, taking the stairs two at a time. He seems happy and my guess is that he has just had a baby. I try to keep up with him, but it's no use. He exits the stairwell at the second floor: maternity. I care little that I guessed right. I slow down, trying not to distress myself with the image of someone in the operating room finding the drawing I slipped under Anna's sheet and laughing right now.

And then I wonder if I should call Anna's brother in Florida.

By the time I reach the third floor and push open the doors into the neurology ward, I am out of breath. I need to see Anna.

The ward seems busier than a few hours ago; it's foolish for me to be here so early. I retreat to the post-op waiting room, with hours still to massacre. But there are people in here. I've entered the room too purposefully to then turn

— 139 —

around and leave without appearing rude, so I sit down in one of the available steel-blue vinyl armchairs.

"Be still," a Chinese woman says to her daughter who is restlessly flopping about on the arm of her chair.

"I've never seen anything like it," says a woman with red hair, dressed in baggy pants and a tank top, her arms freckled and firm. She snuggles into the arm of the woman beside her who is of similar age but has cropped dark hair. The dark-haired woman brushes the redhead's arm in consolation. From their conversation I garner that their friend had an epileptic fit and has been transferred to neurology to see a specialist. They caress one another for comfort, and I wonder if they are lovers or if they have simply been thrown together by events. I slouch down in my chair, trying not to stare at them.

A sporty man enters and sits down beside the Chinese woman and her squirming daughter. They say nothing, and my guess is that their son has been in a bicycle accident. I don't know why this seems the most likely scenario, but it does. The potential for drama is as obvious as a soap opera.

I try to picture Gottlieb now, wielding the jigsaw and then removing a small section of the bone from my wife's skull. But I have difficulty with this.

"You can't go the whole distance," Christine once said to me on a night out when we were celebrating something, I can't remember what. I know for certain it was while she was still on the pill. It might have been a celebration of a new client contract or perhaps the first anniversary of our affair. She had been referring, as I later discovered, to my designs, not to our relationship, but the undertones of the comment had touched a nerve.

"What the fuck is that supposed to mean?" I asked, and took a sip from my wine, wanting to go home to Anna.

"Hey . . ." Christine said, hurt. She slumped back in her chair, and I leaned forward, shunted my chair closer to the table, and took her hand, which she immediately snatched away. We had been discussing a design I'd done for an insurance company—a graphic whose umbrella image I was proud of.

"I'm sorry, but I don't understand," I said, reaching across the table for her hand.

She sulked, but I stroked her hand until she softened.

"All I meant was, I thought maybe you were holding something back. And you do. There's always something you hold back."

"There are commercial constraints, you know that," I said.

"But that's not what I mean. I don't know how else to say it. You hold back," she said, and sipped her expensive Barolo with what felt like resentment. I was convinced that she wanted more, that she hated me for not leaving Anna, and that she was punishing me. After dinner I made love to her in her kitchen and made a point of not holding back in any sense. But what I think she really was pointing to is what I'm sensing for myself in this waiting room, what I've been experiencing over the past month. I'm not capable of going the whole distance even now, with my wife; instead, I've been obsessed about my conscience, my confession. In case she lives? In case she dies? Either way, who would that serve? Only me.

I think of the bone flap being cut from Anna's head and being slid like a snug puzzle piece out of its place in her skull. The dura mater, the membrane that protects her brain, is now exposed. I wonder what they will do with the bone, where they will place it so as not to damage it or lose it.

"You're such a coward, Mike," Anna had said to me when we had returned from the hospital after spending the night at Sasha's side. By morning my daughter's dehydration was in check. The Egyptian desert was still in Anna's hair, still on my skin.

"What?"

Anna threw down her handbag and walked to the back door and pushed it open. The fresh April air cleared the stale winter from our house.

"What?" I repeated.

She turned back to me and I could see her skin go mottled with approaching tears: "Coward."

"What are you talking about?" I couldn't stop thinking about Hamada and the sounds outside our tent.

"When Sasha asked you if you were angry with her," she said. I was taken aback. Sasha had wept when she woke up and saw us there, and had begged for forgiveness.

"She's alive," I said harshly, incensed by the idea that I should have disciplined my daughter in those circumstances.

"But she was asking you, for once, directly, to be angry with her, to show her you had emotion of some kind in you," Anna said, as I felt the rawness turn in my throat. "She wanted you to be angry with her. Don't you get it?"

I didn't get it.

It was a few weeks later that I met Christine.

I strain to feel time passing. Objects appear in the room as though I've drawn them myself. I am stalled in so much rawness that I am all blood and veins and muscle, a sinewy flank of uncooked meat.

I touch the pocket of my shirt and am relieved that I still have my Staedtler. I look around for something to draw on. All I find is the discarded business section of today's *Globe and Mail*. It will have to do.

"Interesting . . . What is it?"

Fred has come up behind me and is looking over my shoulder. I quickly cover the sketch and wonder how long he has been standing there. The Chinese family has gone; the two women are both reading magazines.

"Another international sign, eh, Dad?" he says through a grin that slices off a sliver of laughter. "Have you been sitting here the whole time?" he asks.

I look at my watch. "There's only another hour or so," I say, surprised at how time has passed.

"They'll probably finish early. That's why I came now."

He is so believing, so trusting of how things function in the world.

"This hospital has had some of the lowest MRSA rates in the province," he says, imagining he's reassuring me.

I think about the tiny endoscope that Gottlieb is navigating past the protective layers of brain tissue, steady-steady-hands-that-will-not-slip-and-cut, as he separates the two lobes of Anna's brain on his way towards the arteries and the ultimate goal.

"Wake up, Fred," I say.

"Excuse me?"

And I know that I've pricked the little boy who doesn't like to be challenged in any way, the boy who, on his first solo flight down the high slide in the playground told his mother that she was the one who was frightened and that he would never be.

Did he really think they'd finish early? Fred might be the most fragile of us all, I realize.

We sit in silence. The yellow paint on the wall is cracked and blistering like our failed imaginations.

"Seeing anyone these days?" I ask with as gentle a tone as I can muster.

He looks at me, suspicious, before he nods.

"Nothing like a good distraction," I say, nudging him with my elbow like some pathetic teammate. He shakes his head and looks away, his shoulder edging me out slightly.

I am sorry for what I've done. The image of my mother in her coffin—the tiny head, the shrunken chest cavity, the shock of the stroke still clear on her twisted face despite the mortician's careful work—leads me to take my son's hand.

I breathe in deeply again. Dr. Gottlieb will be trying to secure control of the blood flow in and out of the aneurysm. He knows how easily it can rupture. He is preparing it for clipping.

"Fred," I say, squeezing his hand. He turns towards me.

"Fred," I repeat.

"What's so special about you, then?" he asks.

I let go of his hand.

"It's not like you've ever done anything—" He stops himself and shakes his head. He checks his watch and looks around, craning his neck to see out into the corridor.

I take another deep breath.

"Do you ever fantasize about things, Fred?" He looks at me as though I might be perverted. "I mean, do you ever dream of things you want, like a job, a house, a car, a lover . . . I don't know, anything. Do you fantasize about having them, imagine yourself with them, and get some sort of private joy from that?" He still looks confounded.

"I used to lie in bed at night, before I met your mother, and I used to picture myself in the future—sometimes just the near future, like the next weekend and the perfect woman I'd meet; or two years on when I'd be having a gallery show of my work. I used to pretend that I was being interviewed by a magazine journalist about a particular commission I'd just done, or about winning awards and giving speeches, thanking my parents for making David the banker and me the creative one."

Fred's reaction is still impossible to discern. He looks like me at that age. But if he shifts his lips towards a smile, he instantly becomes Anna. I want him to smile, to react somehow, to stop me.

"But I don't fantasize about the things I want anymore. Do you?"

"Yes, I do," he says, but still doesn't smile.

"Like what?"

"Like fantasizing that if and when Mom wakes up she'll be completely fine," he says. "I'm going to check with Rosie." He rises abruptly and walks out.

I close my eyes and try to picture a year from now with Anna; she is well and we are on a trip somewhere—the Caribbean, or Italy, or even Indonesia. When did I actually stop this little game? When did fantasies become so proven never to come true that it hurt to have them?

I see us now, in this yellow-grey corridor of illness with death's door ajar, creaking on its hinge.

The dome of the aneurysm in Anna's brain has likely now been punctured with a needle and carefully drained to ensure that blood doesn't continue to fill it up. Once the clip is in place, the retractors holding the brain lobes apart are removed and the tissue gently unfolds towards the centre, disturbed but intact.

But where is the bone flap? Lost? Hidden amongst soiled swabs and discarded tongs?

No, it is there, placed gently in sterilized gauze, safely on the tray. Now it's being unwrapped and levered into its crook. Titanium plates cover the fissures and, here, the screws that will secure them to the skull are put in place. The needle that sutures the muscles and skin back together is tough but thin as it pierces through the fabric of my wife's head. I see the ribbon of gauze dressing that the nurse is slowly unravelling over the wound; she will wrap it once, twice, many more times around Anna's head, and my wife will resemble a turbaned Egyptian nomad.

TWELVE

"You're an asshole!"

Charlotte's face is nearly mauve with anger. I don't understand all that has just happened, what it is exactly that we have been told. I don't think I can feel anything as I watch my children react to the news. But my bottom lip is the Geiger counter of the distress that is no doubt taking hold of me, ticking in millisecond beats.

"I realize you're upset," Fred says to Charlotte calmly, in his doctor's voice.

"Go back to your own patients—you're probably more compassionate with them!" Charlotte shouts.

"Stop it, stop it!" Sasha mumbles, also trembling, her tears more timid than Charlotte's. I can do or say nothing to help these three. Gottlieb has spoken a series of words. I have followed their trail to these children, who are reacting for me. One of the words was "complication." *Complication during the surgery.* I have followed that word to Charlotte's distraught face, and I slowly realize what is happening. Charlotte has comprehended immediately what the rest of us have not yet clocked. She believes that the complication experienced in surgery might well result in her mother becoming a vegetable.

"The bone flap."

Dr. Gottlieb pronounced it mechanically, as he stood in his surgery greens in his small consulting room. The Hunt and Hess assessment before the surgery determined that Anna did not have subarachnoid hemorrhage, and her symptoms pointed to a low risk. In normal circumstances, the bone flap is replaced during the craniotomy. Dr. Gottlieb had fully expected to be able to do so in this case as well. But during Anna's surgery, he detected larger swelling in the area than they had anticipated, and the possibility of infection. Gottlieb's other key words were "pressure" and "damage." I slowly began to understand that normal procedure could have caused increased pressure on the brain, resulting in damage that could be as severe as a stroke.

"The bone flap was not replaced," said Dr. Gottlieb to the four of us standing stone-faced in his office. And now that my senses are returning, I can remember his words in their precise order: "But we expect to do so within seven days, after the swelling has been reduced. It's a precaution."

"You're kidding, right?" said Charlotte.

"Char, please," said Fred, embarrassed and trying to keep his professional composure. "It's not uncommon, right?" His tone contained a plea to Gottlieb.

"It's not common, but it does happen. The methods for preserving the bone flap sterilized and intact are exceptional. She's through the worst of it now. She's in recovery. You can see her within the hour."

Dr. Gottlieb stood silent. I could see from his face that he thought his duty was done, and that the people in his office should be grateful that he saved this woman's life and they should now leave him alone. He told us he knew we had a lot to discuss and, guiding us towards the door, said that the nurse would let us know when we could see Anna. We stumbled out of the consulting room like lost tourists.

There have been times in the past when I have seen people in wheelchairs, in vegetative states, when I accidentally have said "sorry" out loud, in a moment of uncontrolled there-but-for-the-grace-of-God empathy, or fear. Anna was superstitious about accidents, though, and would not discuss with me her wishes, not the "do not resuscitate" of a living will, nor the organ donor registry, which she found morbid. The kind of outcome that Charlotte fears is not something I have prepared for.

Perhaps Charlotte has overreacted.

But if she hasn't, my trembling bottom lip tells me I have not equipped myself sufficiently for this outcome. Until now I have not considered what it is that my wife wants. I remember what she said to Susan that day when I overheard them in the kitchen: "I won't be like her. I won't."

What is a mind?

While Charlotte and Fred argue like husband and wife in the waiting room, I am like the child with my hands over my ears. I close my eyes. Come on, come on.

And there, it's faint, but . . . She is on a hillside. She is wearing a short, colourful skirt. I hear birds: a parrot's caw and the twirp of a small red-beaked, turquoise Roller. A Dollarbird. We are in Indonesia. The hill is terraced, and her tight cotton vest makes my wife's back a curve of crimson against the jade paddies. I walk towards her. She's barely more than a girl, and so I look down at my own hands and see that they are not marked by years of futile, meaningless work. They are strong, smooth.

"Mike, this is where we will raise our children," she says softly, with a clarity that is youthful and wise all in one. "Over there, see that land, down below the temple?" she says, and I follow her slim, firm arm to her fingertip and out toward the next hill, where the shimmering, terraced rice fields are like a stretched, swollen Greek amphitheatre. "I've asked them if we can build there," and she unfolds a set of architectural plans she has been holding in her other hand. These are indecipherable to me with their elaborate lines and foreign characters, but Anna seems to know exactly what they all mean. "It's important that the main room faces the sea—this way," and she points again.

"What will we do here?" I ask.

"We'll raise them properly; we'll learn how to cultivate our land; we'll grow old with grace," she says, and her voice is like a wind I want to lie down beneath. "And you'll do your art," she adds. At this I stop myself. The ego's interception of the fantasy has made it all feel contrived.

What is it that I have wanted?

"Dad," Sasha says as she touches my arm. "Come, sit down."

She leads me to the couch. Fred and Charlotte are nowhere to be seen, and I am embarrassed, because I know I have been standing in silence for too long.

"Is Charlotte okay?" I ask her sister. I don't sit down. Sasha shrugs. Her hazel eyes are moist and red. She stands with me, but looks towards the couch.

"She's okay."

"But she—"

"She's worried."

"We all are, but—"

"She's got stuff going on too." Sasha shrugs again, looks at me and finally sits down. "She wanted to tell Mom stuff before the operation, and I told her she shouldn't."

My stomach lurches. I remain standing. "Tell her what stuff?" I ask.

"Stuff," she says sadly.

I examine her face to see where she bears the weight of stuff, where the pain of what she knows about her parents resides. Her cheeks are not drawn; her eyes don't droop; her lips are full and sure. It could be that my youngest child is not marked in any way by my failings.

"Tell me," I say. She looks up at me, and in her cheek is a tinge of regret. "Tell me," I repeat.

"Charlotte lost her job." She takes a breath. "A couple of weeks ago. She didn't want anyone to know because she felt humiliated."

I don't know what's worse: the fact that I'm relieved it isn't about me, or the fact that I do not feel more stirred by my daughter's suffering.

"What happened?" I manage to say. I remember her casual clothes, the jeans and T-shirt when I picked her up for lunch. Why did she have me meet her there and not at home? How did I become so heartless, so unforgiving in their eyes? I think about this morning and my insistence that she should get a new car.

"She fell out, big time, with her boss, and after months of torturing her, he found a way to fire her." Sasha grabs my arm. "You can't let on that you know. She'd kill me, Dad, please."

"But . . ." and I am slipping into a cold gulf.

"Sit," Sasha says.

I do as I'm told.

"Fred has gone to find out more about the bone flap," she says. "They said it really wasn't that unusual, it happens sometimes." She fidgets, crosses her legs, scratches her wrist. Sasha's body choreographs her distress. "I don't know why Charlotte flew off like that." She scratches her wrist again, uncrosses her legs. "I'm scared."

I wrap my arms around her and hold on tight. "It's all going to be okay," I say, as I rub her back and she starts to cry. I feel the tiny eruptions up my daughter's spine, the heaving of her breath in my hands.

"The thought of losing either of you . . ." she whispers, but it gets caught in her throat.

"Sshhh . . ." I offer, and stroke her back.

"Oh, never mind," she says, composing herself, wiping her nose on my shirt.

"Darling, please, if you want to talk about—"

"No, it's fine." She straightens up.

"You've been worried about losing us?"

She takes tissue from her pocket and shakes her head. "More about you losing each other."

I am momentarily confused, and then the shame rushes back in.

"Mom told me, a few years ago . . . I wish people would stop telling me things," she tries to joke, and blows her nose again.

"What did Mom tell you?"

She shakes her head, fixes her hair quickly with her hands, scratches her wrist again.

"Please," I say, not wanting to speak before I am certain, but feeling a rising relief that perhaps everyone, even Anna, already knows, and that my family has been more gracious than I have.

"You know," she says.

"I do?" My cheeks are on fire.

Leave me alone, Christine finally said, one spring day, when I called, late, desperate, begging to see her after telling her only a week earlier that I was devoted to Anna and that we couldn't continue.

"Mom's affair."

No air. A rush of sharp blood to my chest.

My mind slips into reverse, scrambling to find an image that corresponds to these words.

"I know, she told me you didn't want to talk about it," Sasha says.

My burning cheeks begin to twitch as I engage my lips to play a role I haven't rehearsed. "When did she tell you?"

"A few years ago, way after it happened."

Way after it happened.

Again my mind rushes to calculate, to add up and sub-tract where in the calendar of Christine this might fall. Should I be relieved? But relief is not supposed to feel like sharp metal churning below my ribs.

"And what did she say exactly?"

"Sorry, Dad, if you don't want to talk about it . . ." she waves her hand, as if to clear the air of unease.

"No, no, I do," and I have to lick my dry, lying lips to stop them from sticking together.

"She didn't say much, just that it's what can happen in relationships and that you and she were just ordinary people who sometimes found it hard to be together, like everyone else."

"Of course."

No, it's not relief I feel. What's raging in my ribs is more complicated than that, and it includes an untender lust, an arousing image of my wife straddling a faceless man. I rub my palms hard against my brow. Sasha touches my arm.

"Dad, I'm sorry, you didn't need me to bring that up. I'm sorry."

And when I look up I can see the weight of stuff on her face that I couldn't see before. The slight downturn of her mouth and the trembling lip that resembles mine after all.

"Not a problem," I say, drawing her nearer to me. "We're past that. Now, I wonder if it isn't time to go in and see her."

"She's probably still sleeping," she says.

"You go check, let me know."

She doesn't budge.

"Please, darling."

Sasha stands and hesitates, but I will her with all my might to leave. She eventually walks off. I have no feeling in my feet, but there's a tingling at the end of my earlobes. And Anna is still unconscious.

I despise her.

I slouch back on the couch. It hurts. I stand up. This is worse. I sit back down, but on the floor this time, with my back pressed up against the couch. *Way after it happened.* I stand up again and begin pacing. The water cooler gurgles. I raise my foot, whack it with my heel and walk out of the room.

When you fucked him . . . you opened your legs and guided him into you and you fucked him. Or was it your ass you raised, pumping it, pink and spanked . . . you fucking fucked him . . .

There are so many people in the ward—the two women visiting their epileptic friend; the Chinese family is back and waiting for news on their son; the nurse with the beard and tattoos; the fee-fi-fo-fum throng of illness. I walk towards her room at the far end of the hallway. I picture myself ripping the tubes from her arms, delicately lifting her head, but then letting it fall back—hard— against the stiff hospital pillow.

In the corridor there is a door marked Janitor. I try the handle, surprised when it turns. I don't even check around me to see if anyone is watching. I enter the walk-in cupboard packed full of cleaning solutions, bleaches, liquids in large plastic bottles marked with skull and crossbones. My legs buckle and I slouch down against some giant rolls of paper towel, accidentally knocking over a spray bottle of tile cleaner in the process.

There's an elaborate floor polisher in front of me, and my shoe rubs against the felt of its polishing disc. I try to focus on the construction of this disc, the mechanics of the machine—imagining intricate pulleys and levers, where the engine clicks in, and how it propels the pad over the floor. I realize I know nothing about how things like this are built; not even the mop, there—the long strands of cotton strings that slop up the puke, shit, and blood of this ward and then get squeezed into the trough that rings out the water. I don't understand the simplest of mechanisms.

Who had been Anna's lover? Another teacher? A man whose words flowed to please her, tease her, whispering as he entered her? I picture them and my stomach churns. Why did she stop seeing him?

My head slumps forward. I am embarrassed by the janitor's uniform, which hangs on the door to my right, as though it is observing me at my most ridiculous. Which version of our past has Charlotte been privy to, after all? Anna felt no need to confess; she wasn't concerned about leaving me with false memories of my wife.

Eventually I focus on the crisp cobalt blue coveralls hanging on the hook. They look as though they would fit me and I consider putting them on.

And then I am back in Bali, on that terraced hillside with Anna, her back to me, her arm outstretched as she points towards something down in the the terraced, jade valley. I think it's our home, the place where we will grow old together.

"We're ordinary people," she says, as she turns and looks at me. I see that her face is as beautiful as ever, her language unflawed, no sign of any damage from the operation. Her head is perfectly shaped. Strands of her hair are rising and falling in the breeze like the shoots of new rice that make the hill an undulating green ribbon that we're carefully balancing on.

THIRTEEN

If they've changed the bed then someone will have left the drawing for her on the side table, or it's been bundled up in the soiled sheets and will be laundered with them, its ink bleeding into the cheap cotton.

When I arrive at the door to the room she is surrounded. Rosie is arranging something near the bed; the children are gathered in a semi-circle. I catch sight of my wife's face framed by the white gauze turban and almost do not recognize her. My eyes flicker to the ventilator, the IV, the tubes in her arm. When I look back up at her face I see that her eyes are sunken, with dark circles underneath, as though she's been beaten.

She sees me. The children notice the shift in her gaze, and turn around, their tear-stained faces puffy like wet cardboard. I force myself closer, then almost skip towards them in a jolt of confusion. Anna looks at me with what could be concern, but I smile.

"Sweetheart," I say, and sweep my fingers under the pillow near her head, feeling for the paper, before bending my face to hers, resting it against her cheek without pressure. The gauze around her head is slightly moist, and I smell something like mould masked by disinfectant and a lemony balm. I stay longer than feels appropriate and do another sweep with my fingers.

"Dad," Charlotte says, sounding irritated. I push myself up on my hands and glare at her, then look back at Anna, whose eyes search mine. I don't know how to look at her. She opens her mouth as if to speak, but doesn't.

"Has she said anything?" I ask Fred as I stand up straight.

"Her throat is sore as hell, I bet, from the breathing tube," he says, "so I doubt she'll want to for a while, but they did neurological tests in the ICU, and they've found no evidence of damage. If she's here, it means she's answered their questions, like 'what is your name' and 'what day is it?' over and over. So, she can speak to us, she just hasn't felt up to it yet."

I'm amazed by the depth of my relief.

Anna stares blankly, and I wonder if Fred is right. Does she understand us? I want them to leave us alone now. Please go, I repeat, over and over in my head, as Charlotte strokes her mother's hand. The knuckles of my daughter's fingers flow smoothly, up and down. Each articulation of the bones is purposeful, almost dangerous. I remember all the times I told Charlotte how crucial it was to be self-sufficient, no matter what she chose to do and how she had to work hard and not be dependent. But that was not real life I was talking about. I keep my eyes on her knuckles.

"I'll be back in a few minutes," I say. They glower at me. "And then I'd like to be alone with her. Is that okay?" I notice that Rosie has disappeared from the room. Sasha nods at me first, then Charlotte and Fred nod in unison. I kiss Anna on the cheek and pick up my briefcase from the floor.

I walk briskly out of the ward, down the elevator, through the crowded lobby and onto the street.

I find a patch of grass near the corner of Queen and Church streets, in front of the hostel for men in a wing of the Metropolitan United Church. I open my briefcase, take out paper and a new Staedtler, and I begin.

After a few strokes, I falter. I look around me. There is a group of young men gathered on the corner, all of them with their belts so loose their pants sit midway down their asses. A woman pushing a shopping cart loaded with her valuables passes me and glares, paranoid no doubt that I am sketching her. I'm sorry, I think to myself. I'm sorry.

A young man goes by—he's attractive, in jeans and a white T-shirt: a simple, well-honed look. He is the shape I still like to imagine myself to be, even after so many years. He is the body double for my stale ambitions.

More people pass me. I try to determine what makes one different from the other. It isn't their sex: many of them, male and female, are dressed the same. It isn't their race: there are black, white, brown and pink faces, all with the same unhappy glare. Is it their minds? No, not that either.

I begin again.

In the figure that takes shape, I begin to understand how my own mark has been dull and feeble for so long.

I sketch and shadow.

When I'm finished, I look up at the clock in the church tower. I've been gone for over an hour. I fold up the drawing and tuck it into my pocket. My legs feel limber as I stand and hurry across the grass.

Once back in the neurological ward I realize I've left my briefcase on the grass, but never mind. I see the children down the hall, talking to Rosie, taking in her instructions like good kindergarten pupils. I duck into the room unnoticed.

Anna's eyes are closed. I think about the bone flap that lies sterilized in the surgeon's jar, and the gaping hole that exposes what it is that keeps my wife alive.

My imagination has been poor. I touch the paper in my pocket. I take it out and delicately unfold it.

She opens her eyes. "How are you feeling?" I ask. I'm fully aware it's a stupid question, but I mean it. I want to know. I want to hear her voice.

"Mmm," she murmurs. There's a voice there, and I hope there will be clarity and precision to the words that come. She touches her neck and tries to smile, but I see that she's in pain.

"Anna," I say quietly, as I lay out the sheet of paper and look again at what I have done.

It is a different kind of shape—a shape without bulk. One that I hope holds truth in its throat, like the bone of song or the cartilage of a scream.

"For you," I say, as I hold up the paper, smoothing out its creases, careful with its edges.

"Yes," she says. "Yes, I see."

ACKNOWLEDGEMENTS

Some of the medical information and inspiration for this book came from Paul Broks' beautiful and disturbing *Into the Silent Land*. Further technical details on confabulation were drawn from William Hirstein's *Brain Fiction*, among other books.

Thanks to the Canada Council for financial support during the writing of this novel and to the School of Humanities and Social Sciences at the University of East London for research funding.

It was a privilege to work with Aleksandar Maćašev, who patiently listened to me during innumerable Skype calls and shaped my wild abstractions into Mike's beautiful illustrations. Thanks to Stephanie Young for reading and believing in it from the start; to Jackie Kaiser for the title; and to Attila Berki for copyediting. Thanks to Anne Collins at Random House Canada for her spirit, support and commitment.

This book has two godfathers: John Berger, who sometimes ends our phone conversations with, "Now I put my hand on your shoulder and turn you back to your work"; and the wonderful Andrew Kidd, to whom I am deeply grateful for his sensitive attention, every step along the way.

A NOTE ABOUT THE TYPE

Vital Signs is set in Bell MT, created in 1931 by the Monotype Company. It is a facsimile of an original typeface cut for John Bell by Richard Austin in 1788. Used in Bell's newspaper, *The Oracle*, it was regarded by Stanley Morison as the first English Modern face. Although inspired by French punchcutters of the time, the face is less severe than the French models and is now classified as Transitional.

BOOK DESIGN BY CS RICHARDSON